FEATURE**SPOTLIGHT**

This Week in Advertising...

The Adman:
Brock Maddox

His New Campaign:
Adams Temp Services—when you
unexpectedly need a new secretary

Well, we've all finally learned who was behind the information leaks at Maddox Communications. But could anyone have guessed it
was CEO Brock Maddox's own assistant? Seems
the sweet-looking Elle Linton was hiding quite a
lot. Including the fact that she is Athos Koteas's
illegitimate granddaughter. See   thos
has never claimed her as   s to
wonder why she   ths
to betray M   st
discovered sr   -
lationship with

Is Brock Maddc   able to overcome
this latest crush   ews in what has already
been a trying year for his advertising company?
The Maddox family has weathered tougher
storms...we think. But with the news that Brock
is marrying Elle...well, we have to wonder what
else is going on behind the scenes. Why would
Maddox marry the woman who spied on his
beloved company? Unless...that very woman is
about to be the mother of a Maddox heir?

Dear Reader,

Have you ever been in a situation where you had to compromise your integrity for the sake of someone else's life? What if someone else would actually die if you didn't compromise your honor? The "shero" in *CEO's Expectant Secretary* is put in this untenable situation. In order for her mother to get the medical treatments she needs, Elle Linton must steal secrets from her boss. That's bad enough, but what if she falls for her boss? Can you imagine the angst you would feel if you were put in that situation?

This story was full of vibrant emotions that pulled me from one end of the spectrum to the other. The betrayal the hero experiences, the morning sickness Elle suffers, their struggle to make a life together…

I was thrilled to write the resolution to this exciting multi-author series. I loved exploring Elle and Brock's journey and sharing a little about the wonderful couples who found love before them, and I hope you'll enjoy this dramatic conclusion to KINGS OF THE BOARDROOM!

Best Wishes,

Leanne Banks

www.leannebanks.com

LEANNE BANKS

CEO'S EXPECTANT SECRETARY

Published by Silhouette Books

America's Publisher of Contemporary Romance

Special thanks and acknowledgment to Leanne Banks
for her contribution to the
Kings of the Boardroom miniseries.

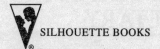

SILHOUETTE BOOKS
®

Recycling programs
for this product may
not exist in your area.

ISBN-13: 978-0-373-73031-5

CEO'S EXPECTANT SECRETARY

Copyright © 2010 by Harlequin Books S.A.

For questions and comments about the quality of this book please contact us
at Customer_eCare@Harlequin.ca.

Visit Silhouette Books at www.eHarlequin.com

Printed in U.S.A.

Books by Leanne Banks

Silhouette Desire

*The Royal Dumonts
†The Billionaires Club
**The Medici Men

LEANNE BANKS

is a *New York Times* and *USA TODAY* bestselling author who is surprised every time she realizes how many books she has written. Leanne loves chocolate, the beach and new adventures. To name a few, Leanne has ridden on an elephant, stood on an ostrich egg (no, it didn't break), gone parasailing and indoor skydiving. Leanne loves writing romance because she believes in the power and magic of love. She lives in Virginia with her family and four-and-a-half-pound Pomeranian named Bijou. Visit her Web site at www.leannebanks.com.

This book is dedicated to all the fabulous authors of the KINGS OF THE BOARDROOM books and my family—Betty Minyard, Karen Minyard, Jane Poff, Tony Banks, Adam Banks, Alisa Kline, Kevin Kline, Richard Turner, Amy Turner, Mason Turner, Julia Turner, Phillip Poff, Jennifer Little, Rex Little, Asher Little and Emily Pierce.

Prologue

He couldn't sleep.

Brock Maddox looked down at the woman on the bed beside him. Her eyelids were closed, her dark lashes hiding the warm sensuality of her blue eyes. Her brown hair splayed across his pillow and her wicked, wonderful lips were swollen from the lovemaking they'd shared just an hour ago.

The soft sheet sloped over her full breasts, which she'd tried to keep hidden; the dusky rose of a nipple peeked above the white cotton. His fingertips knew the feel of everything beneath that sheet—every rib, the curve of her waist and lower still, the wet, velvet secrets that encased him, stroked him and plunged him into another world.

Elle Linton had captured his attention the first time she'd walked into his office for a job interview. Fearing she might present a distraction, he'd chosen a different woman who had subsequently decided to quit just one month later. Elle was the natural next choice.

By far the most observant assistant he'd ever had, she had quickly taken note of his every preference, from his favorite sandwich and soothing music to who was allowed to interrupt him and who wasn't. A few late nights with sandwiches had progressed to wine and gourmet delivery. A couple of innocent brushes against her body had left him hard with longing.

He'd begun to smell her perfume in his sleep. He'd noticed her gaze lingering on him and seen the wanting in her eyes—he should have resisted. He remembered the night everything had changed between them as if it were five minutes ago....

Six o'clock. He should tell Elle she could leave, he thought, opening the door to his office. She had been standing right outside. Giving a smothered sound of surprise, she dropped the files on the floor.

"Sorry," he said, bending down at the same time she did. "Didn't mean to startle you."

Her perfume rose to his nostrils and he felt that same seductive tug. The one he always pushed aside. She stumbled and he instinctively pulled her against him.

Her eyes met his and irresistible electricity crackled between them. He was achingly aware of her breasts against his chest and the sensation of her thighs on either side of his leg as he held her upright.

"Sorry," she whispered, her gaze holding his.

She wore a black pencil skirt with a back vent, her legs were bare, her feet in a pair of black heels that made it difficult to tear his gaze from her backside throughout the day. If she were another woman, he would lower his head and take her mouth. He would pull her blouse free and slide his hands over her breasts, savoring the touch of her naked skin. If she were another woman, he would pull up her skirt and make her wet with wanting him, then thrust inside her until…

"I should—" he began.

She closed her eyes. "Should. Do you ever get tired of that word?" she asked. "I do."

Her response shocked him and a frustrated chuckle escaped his throat. "Elle…"

She opened her eyes and her gaze spoke to him, making wicked invitations.

"If I were responsible and sane, I would transfer you to another position," he said.

She opened her mouth in protest. "No—"

He put his fingers over her lips. "But I—" He rubbed her lips and she flicked her tongue over his finger. He swore. "Just tell me you want this as much as I do," he said.

She tugged his tie loose and pulled open his shirt, buttons cascading to the floor. "More," she said.

Then he'd pulled her into his arms and carried her upstairs to his private apartment where they'd spent the entire night burning up the bed.

Brock stared down at her as she slept peacefully. His gut knotted at the thought of the preliminary report he'd received from his private investigator. He would meet with the P.I. tomorrow, but the brief text message indicated that Elle might be the person leaking secrets about Maddox Communications to their biggest rival, Golden Gate Promotions.

He hadn't read the text until after they'd made love. Now he was stuck with a nauseating sense of betrayal. Was it true? He would wait for the hard evidence. He would need to see it with his own eyes. Was it possible that the woman who had warmed his heart and his bed for the last several months had secretly been stabbing him in the back?

One

Brock strode down the hallway of the cushy San Francisco North Bay condominium and cynically wondered how Elle could afford such luxury. He paid her well, but not this well. No, he knew exactly how she could afford it, he thought, tightening his jaw. Elle, his assistant—his lover—had sold him out. The time had come for confrontation. Brock wasn't CEO of the top advertising agency in San Francisco for nothing.

With controlled anger, he narrowed his eyes as he knocked on her door on a sunny Saturday morning. He counted as he waited. One. Two. Three. Four. Still in shock that the sweet woman who'd become his mistress had turned out to be a cold-hearted liar, he balled his fist as he waited. Five. Six. Seven.

The door swung open and the woman who had made love to him with no holds barred stared up at him with a pale face and plum lips. Her dark brown hair was sexy-sleep disheveled and her blue eyes rounded in surprise at him.

"Brock," she said, lifting her shoulders in the ivory silk robe she wore. "I thought you wanted to keep our relationship private," she whispered. "Is there a business emergency?"

"You could say that," he said. "I've found out who is selling our secrets."

Alarm shot through her gaze and she shook her head, an expression of dread washing over her face. Her skin paled even more and she covered her mouth. "I'm sorry," she said. "I can't—" She broke off and ran away from him, leaving the door wide open.

Disconcerted, he stared after her. *What the hell?* Stepping inside the small but elegant foyer, he closed the door behind him and walked a few steps down the hallway. He heard the unmistakable sound of Elle losing her breakfast as he glanced at his watch. Despite his overriding fury, he felt a twinge of pity. She hadn't appeared sick when he'd last seen her on Friday.

Minutes later, she came out of the bathroom, still pale. She spotted him as she lifted her hand to her forehead and sighed, looking away. Brock followed her as she walked down the hallway and turned into a moderate-sized kitchen decorated in shades of rust and cream. The contrast of the cream ceramic tile against her cherry-colored toenails emphasized her femininity. He remembered the sight of her naked from head to toe, whispering his name over and over as he made her his, driving both of them into pure pleasure.

He pushed aside the memory. "How long have you

been sick?" he asked as she reached in the refrigerator for a can of ginger ale and poured it into a glass with ice.

"I'm not sick." Her hand shook as she lifted the glass and took a sip. "It's just the mornings—" She broke off and took another sip. "It's nothing really."

Something in her voice tugged at him. Something wasn't right. *Sick. Mornings.* Realization shot through him like a round from a forty-five. He sucked in a quick breath. It wasn't possible, he told himself, yet his gut told him otherwise. His gut told him what he didn't want to know. Brock had learned long ago not to ignore what that churning sensation inside him had to say. It had saved him personally and professionally too many times to count. "You're pregnant," he said.

She closed her eyes and turned away from him.

"Elle," he said, his heart hammering against his rib cage. "Don't lie to me—not this time," he added, unable to keep a touch of cynicism from his voice. "Is it mine?"

Agonizing seconds of silence passed. "Elle," he said.

"Yes," she whispered desperately. "Yes. I'm pregnant with your child."

Brock felt his heart stop in his chest. He swallowed a thousand oaths. The woman who had betrayed him carried his child. He raked his hand through his hair. He'd walked into her building ready to throw the book at her. He still wanted to. No one got the best of Brock Maddox. No one.

He ground his teeth together. He'd protected his family business—he could do no less for his child. His child deserved his name, his history, his everything. There was only one thing to do. "You must marry me."

Elle jerked her head to gape at him. "Absolutely not. You didn't want our relationship to be public. Why would you want things to be different now?"

"Because you're carrying my child. Everything is different now."

Elle took a quick little sip of ginger ale as if to calm herself, then shook her head. "This is crazy. You made it perfectly clear that our relationship was a secret fling." She met his gaze briefly and he glimpsed a stab of pain in her blue eyes before she looked away again.

"If we want to do the right thing for the baby, then we have no choice. We must get married and raise this child together," he said, his jaw clenching with tension. Five minutes ago, he'd been ready to show Elle everything he had against her. He had trusted her. She had betrayed him and his company and he'd wanted to make her pay. His fingers clutched at the envelope full of evidence.

She gnawed at her lip, still avoiding his gaze. "I can't—" She broke off and lifted her chin. "I won't marry you. The pregnancy was unexpected."

He felt a sinking in his gut. "You're not planning to have an abortion."

She met his gaze in shock. "Of course not," she said. "I'll raise this baby on my own." She slid her hand protectively over her abdomen.

"You'll just want unlimited financial support, right?" he asked, unable to check his cynicism.

She narrowed her eyes. "I can take care of this baby

on my own. I don't want anything from you. Do you hear?" she demanded. "Not a thing."

"That's ridiculous," he said. "I can provide—"

"Get out," she said in a low, firm voice.

He blinked at the resolute expression on her face. "Excuse me?"

"Get out," she repeated. "You're not welcome here."

Stunned at the strength of her response, he shook his head. He hesitated only because she looked so fragile and he didn't want to upset her more. "I'll leave," he said. "But I'll be back." He strode out of the condo, already formulating a plan. He was, after all, known as the man with a plan. Always.

Elle held her breath as she watched Brock Maddox leave. As soon as she heard the front door close, she finally exhaled. The room seemed to turn sideways and she felt the alarming sense of her knees weakening. She quickly grasped onto the counter, her hands shaking as she set down her glass.

She just needed to get to a chair, she coached herself. If she could just sit down for a moment.… On wobbly legs, she made her way to a barstool and slid onto it. She took a breath, praying for her head to stop spinning.

How had he found out? She'd been so careful when she'd become Brock's assistant and been forced to spy on him. She'd been so careful—except for that minor matter of going to bed with her boss and having a scorching affair with him. Her intentions had been honorable. She'd needed the money for her mother's cancer treatments.

Her grandfather had offered her a way to do that while accomplishing his own, less honorable goal.

When she'd first started working for Brock, she'd told herself to treat the job the same way a man would. Compartmentalize. She would do an excellent job for Maddox Communications as she ferreted secrets for her grandfather, Athos Koteas. Elle felt a bitter taste form in the back of her throat. In one way or another, she had spent her entire life at the mercy of a powerful man. Elle might not like the cards that had been dealt, but she would damn well play them to the best of her ability. She wouldn't let her mother die as a result of her pride or a misplaced sense of ethics in a business completely without ethics.

The only thing she hadn't counted on was Brock. Meeting him had made her feel as if she were in an earthquake that was rocking her to her core. She'd never intended to be attracted to him, let alone go to bed with him. And she'd never dreamed she would fall for him.

Elle heard the sound of soft footsteps in the hallway and glanced up to see her mother walk into the kitchen. Though a bit weak and frail, Suzanne seemed to be improving with the help of the experimental cancer treatments. Elle immediately plastered a smile on her face to hide how upset she was over Brock's visit. "Good morning, Mom. Can I fix you some blueberry pancakes for breakfast?" Elle was always looking for a way to keep up her mother's strength and weight.

Her mother shook her head. "Never try to kid a kidder, kiddo. I overheard the whole conversation with Brock. It's obvious that you're in love with the man. I don't want you giving up your chance for happiness because of my illness."

Elle quickly pulled her mother into a hug. "Don't be ridiculous. You and I have always taken care of each other. Besides, I always knew things wouldn't work out long-term with Brock. I just let myself get carried away," she whispered.

"But the baby," her mother said, pulling back, her eyes searching Elle's face. "What are you going to do about the baby?"

"I'm strong," Elle said. "I can take care of myself and my little one." She lifted her hand to her mother's cheek. "You should know. You helped make me strong."

Her mother sighed, her gaze filled with worry. "But, Elle, the man asked you to marry him. Do you know what I would have given for your father to ask me to marry him?"

Elle's stomach clenched. "Brock didn't ask. He issued an order, the same way he would in the office." She shook her head, knowing that everything between her and Brock had changed before he'd walked through her front door. He clearly knew she'd been giving away the company's secrets. He would never forgive her, never trust her. She refused to bring her baby into a marriage of distrust and anger.

Taking a deep breath, she patted her mom's hand. "Come on, now. You and I have more important things to focus on. Like your health, the baby and—" she forced her lips into a determined smile "—blueberry pancakes."

Brock gunned his black Porsche down the freeway. At the speed he was driving, he should have gotten a ticket.

His heart wouldn't stop hammering in his chest. He'd been so ready to slice her to shreds. If he hadn't been intimate with Elle, he would have pursued her legally. She had betrayed him.

He sucked in a sharp, shallow breath. He still couldn't believe he'd trusted her. He still couldn't believe he'd given in to his urge to take her and claim her. She'd been so passionate in his bed. Making love with her had been addictive, had taken him to a totally different level than he'd ever experienced before. He wouldn't admit that to anyone but himself. He needed to go somewhere quiet, somewhere where he could figure out his next step. He was going to be a father.

On impulse, Brock took an exit and drove toward Muir Woods. The huge, mysterious-looking Redwoods called to him. The trees were almost as old as time. What advice would they offer? Not many knew he had a spiritual side, but deep down he did. Too often he'd pushed that element of his being aside because he was the one who'd been left in charge of Maddox Communications. Regardless of the odds, regardless of his adversaries, he was the one who had to keep it alive.

Brock pulled off the road and got out of his car. The shade of the trees surrounded him with a quiet he longed to feel inside. He took a deep breath, trying to inhale the peace, but his mind was racing at a breakneck speed. Every morning since his father had died, Brock had woken up in warrior mode. Except for a few stolen mornings with Elle. Being with her had provided a secret relief from his everyday pressures. She'd known what he was going through with the company and hadn't questioned the need to keep their affair secret. She'd welcomed him with warmth and passion, and she'd been the only person in his life who hadn't made demands on him. Now he knew why, he thought, bitterness burning through him like acid.

Until now, Brock's priority had been the company's success. Now his world had shifted. Soon enough, he would need to protect a child. In the meantime, he would protect his child's mother, Elle—the woman who had betrayed him and his company.

Brock knew, however, who was behind this. Athos Koteas. His lip curled in distaste. The man would stop at nothing to bring down Maddox Communications. And he had gone too far this time. Athos, the owner of Golden Gate Productions, Maddox Communications' biggest rival, was known as pure poison and would play dirty to get his way.

The peaceful solitude around Brock did nothing to calm his anger, which was only escalating. The time had come for him to confront Athos in person.

Returning to his Porsche, he started the engine and drove to the Koteas house, determined to bring the battle between Golden Gate and Maddox into the open. Ironically, Athos lived in Nob Hill, not far from Brock's own family home. Brock pulled in front of the large Edwardian mansion with lush cascades of bougainvillea, but the beauty was lost on him.

Climbing the steps to the front door, he stabbed the door chime. A moment later, a woman dressed in a black suit answered the door. "Hello. May I help you?"

"I'm here to see Mr. Koteas," Brock said.

"Is he expecting you?"

"He'll see me," Brock said. "My name is Brock Maddox."

The woman looked him over, then guided him to a formal sitting area. But Brock wasn't at all inclined to sit. His anger still burning inside him, he paced the carpet. He heard footsteps and glanced around to see Athos walking toward him. The short, stocky man still had a full head of silver-and-white hair, and a sharp glint in his gaze.

"Good morning, Brock," Athos said, lifting a dark eyebrow. "An unexpected pleasure."

Brock clenched one of his hands into a fist and released it. "Perhaps not. I know you've been trying to destroy Maddox Communications. I recognize that you have very little honor, but I never dreamed you would use your own granddaughter to do your dirty work."

Athos acted confused yet his face tightened. "Granddaughter? What granddaughter?"

"You can forget the pretense," Brock said. "Elle Linton is your granddaughter. But you wouldn't want to make that public, would you? She's illegitimate because your son abandoned her mother."

"It's not unusual for children to disappoint their parents," he said, shrugging. "Elle shows promise. She's intelligent."

"Crafty, like you," Brock said, the knot in his gut pulling tighter. "You don't mind getting anyone dirty as long as you get your way."

"I didn't become a success by avoiding a fight," Athos said, lifting his chin and narrowing his eyes. "You're a successful man, too. You and I are more alike than you think."

Brock felt his blood pressure go through the roof. He clenched his fist again, willing himself not to knock Athos off his almighty perch of pride. "I don't think so. I wouldn't force my grandchild to wallow in the mud for me."

"I didn't force—"

"And her pregnancy, was that part of your plan, too?" Brock goaded the man.

Athos's hard veneer slipped. "Pregnancy?" he said. "What are you talking about?"

"Elle," Brock said. "She's pregnant with my child."

Athos turned pale as he shook his head. "No, she wasn't supposed to—" He continued to shake his head, his skin color changing from white to gray as he began to fall.

Brock watched in disbelief, rushing toward the man, catching him as he collapsed. Stunned at the limp body of his adversary, he shook his head. "Call an ambulance!" he yelled. "Mr. Koteas is ill."

Elle rushed through the doors of the emergency room, her heart in her throat. The only other time she could remember being this upset was when she'd learned her mother had cancer. Although Athos had never been affectionate toward her, Elle still felt a debt to him for his financial support of her mother and her.

Brock stepped in front of her as she headed straight for the information desk and she faltered. Her breath hitched at the sight of him, so tall, so strong. Then she remembered what Athos's housekeeper had told her. Brock had been with her grandfather when he'd collapsed.

Brock reached for her and she shrank from him. "You," she said, every cell in her body accusing him. "You're the one who caused this. You caused my grandfather to have a heart attack."

Brock shook his head. "I never would have dreamed he was so fragile." He gently took her arm. "I won't let you handle this alone. I don't want you upset."

"Not upset?" she retorted, pulling her arm away from him. "How could I not be? Do you realize what you've done? I'll never forgive you for this. Never," she said, pushing away from him.

Her stomach in knots, she approached the information desk. "Athos Koteas," she said over the terrible lump in her throat. "Is he—" She broke off, unable to form the words. "How is he?" she whispered.

The nurse gave her a look of sympathy. "Your name?" she asked.

"Elle. Elle Linton," she said, holding her breath.

"Come this way. Mr. Koteas has been asking for you."

Her heart filled with dread, she followed the nurse to the last room on the hallway. Elle looked inside and saw her grandfather hooked up to monitors and tubes. He'd always seemed so strong, so much larger than life when she was a child.

The nurse nodded. "You can go in."

Elle tentatively stepped into the room, moving closer to the bed. Her grandfather's face was pale with strain, his usually neat hair mussed, his eyes closed. The green gown emphasized his ashen complexion. "Athos," she said, because she'd been instructed long ago not to call him grandfather. For a long time, she and her mother had only served to remind Athos of his disappointment in his son.

Her grandfather opened his eyes. "Elle," he said, lifting his hand.

She immediately wrapped both her hands around his. "I'm so sorry about Brock," she said, unable to hide her desperation. "When he called to tell me you were in the hospital, I was horrified that he would go to your house and accuse you." She shook her head. "It's his fault that you had a heart—"

"No, no," Athos said, shaking his head. His eyes were weary. "Brock Maddox is not responsible for my heart problems."

"I don't believe that," she insisted. "If he hadn't shown up at your house—"

Athos gave her hands a feeble squeeze and shrugged. "It would have happened sometime," he said. "It has happened before," he told her, meeting her gaze. "It will happen again."

Confusion and fear trickled through her, the combination burning like acid. "What do you mean? What are you talking about? You've always been strong and healthy."

Athos sighed. "My doctor has told me I don't have much time. I may have been able to fool people that I'm strong, but my heart is very weak."

"Well, surely there's something that can be done. You should get a second opinion."

"Elle," he said in a chiding tone. "I've received only the best care. There's nothing that can be done. The reason I asked you to spy on Maddox is because I wanted to make Golden Gate Promotions solid before..."

Elle's throat clenched and she shook her head. "You're not going to die," she said. "You just need to get your strength back."

Athos's mouth lifted in a sad smile. "I've faced this. You must face it, too," he said as he took a deep breath and closed his eyes. "I'm sorry for getting you involved in my scheme. Brock was right. I shouldn't have asked you to take care of my dirty work."

"Excuse me," the nurse said from behind her. "We'll be moving Mr. Koteas to the Cardiac Care Unit. We need you to return to the waiting room."

Elle quickly kissed her grandfather's cheek and walked to the waiting room. Brock was standing across the room. She was surprised he was still there. A rush of contradictory feelings surged through her. He had become so many things to her—boss, lover, enemy. Father of her child.

Her mind raced back to what her grandfather had told her. He was going to die soon, and her mother's future was uncertain. Was she going to lose the two most important people in her life? Sheer panic squeezed the breath from her lungs. She tried to force herself to breathe, but she couldn't. Her head suddenly felt light and Brock's image swam before her eyes.

"Elle," he said, moving toward her, his face tight with concern. "Elle," he said again and everything went black.

Two

Alarm slammed through Brock as he caught Elle. "Elle," he said, and swore under his breath.

Her eyelids fluttered and she moved her head as if she were trying to shake off her weakness. "Brock," she murmured and shook her head.

"I'm taking you home with me," he said firmly.

"No," she said, shaking her head again. "I shouldn't. I—"

"I won't take no for an answer. You've been hit with too much today. You need to rest without interruption. My home is the best place for that."

Elle sighed and bit her lip, her eyes darkening with flashes of different emotions. "Okay," she said, reluctance in her voice.

Brock tucked Elle into his car and drove to his family home in Nob Hill. He ushered her up the steps to the home of his youth. He spent most of his time in the apartment he'd built at Maddox Communications, but that didn't seem like the right place for Elle, especially in her fragile state.

"You never brought me here before," she said. "It's beautiful."

"I wanted things to stay private with you."

She stopped. "And now?"

He lifted his hand to push a strand of hair from her face. "Now it's different."

"Because of the baby," she said.

"More responsibility is required when a child is involved," he told her. "We can talk more later. Come on in. You need to rest."

He pushed open the door and Anna, his head house-keeper, quickly rushed to the foyer. "Mr. Maddox. How can I help you?"

"Anna, this is Elle Linton. She's had a difficult day. I'd like her to have a chance to rest," he said.

"The blue bedroom?" she suggested. "It's on this floor."

He nodded. "Perfect. Is Mrs. Maddox here today?"

Anna shook her head. "No, sir. I believe your mother is in Paris at the moment."

Thank God, he thought. He wished she would stay there, although he knew she wouldn't. He'd learned long ago that his mother was a heartless woman who'd married his father for money and given him two sons because it was expected of her. Since his father had died, she'd tried to find ways to extract money from Brock and his brother Flynn.

He guided Elle toward the blue bedroom at the back

of the house. "I think you'll be comfortable here," he said as Anna drew the shades and pulled down the covers.

"You know I can't stay," she said, sinking onto the bed. "I'm only here because it's been such a difficult, crazy day."

"I know," he said, but his intentions were entirely different. "Anna, can you please get Miss Linton some water? Perhaps juice," he added.

Elle shook her head. "Water will be just fine." She closed her eyes and took a deep breath, then opened them again as if she were fighting her weariness.

"Kick off your shoes and rest," he said after Anna left. "It will be best for you and the baby."

She took off her shoes and lay down on the mattress. "This is just for a little while," she warned him, her eyelids growing heavier with each second.

"Put your feet under the covers," he told her. "Your water will be on the nightstand. You need to rest, Elle. Close your eyes."

Closing her eyes, she sighed. "Just for a little while," she said.

He watched her and within seconds, her breathing slid into a regular rhythm. Unable to force his gaze from her, he stared. The sight of her in his home did something crazy to his insides. He'd thought his heart was dead after his fiancée left him. He'd planned to keep things low-key with Elle. Knowing she was expecting his child, though, changed everything, even his resentment toward her because she'd betrayed him.

He needed to move quickly. Brock had never been more certain of the right thing to do in his life. Taking in the sight of her lovely face, her parted lips inhaling even, measured breaths, he felt his resolve solidify.

Forcing himself to look away from her, he left the room and called his publicist.

Hours later, Elle awakened to a semidark room. The bed and furnishings were unfamiliar. Uncertainty rushed through her as she rose to her elbows, trying to shake off her grogginess. Then she saw Brock seated across the room with an electronic book reader in his hands.

He glanced up at her. "Okay?"

Everything came back to her—the terrible scene in the kitchen with Brock, her grandfather's heart attack. Panic raced through her. She threw off the covers and swung her feet to the floor. "I need to check on my mother and grandfather."

Brock was beside her in seconds, putting his hands gently on her shoulders as if to steady her. "Already done. Your mother is making an early night of it. She said you should do the same. You've been too stressed lately. Athos is resting comfortably in the CCU. If he continues to improve, he'll be moved to a regular room on the cardiac floor tomorrow."

Despite all the tension between her and Brock, she couldn't deny her relief at his touch and the reassurance of his confident voice. "You're sure?" she asked. "You're sure they're okay."

"I'm sure," he said, then glanced at the clock. "It's late, but you're probably hungry."

Elle gasped when she saw the time. "Oh, my goodness, it's nine-thirty. I can't believe I slept that long. I need to get home."

"Not tonight," he said firmly.

"What do you mean?"

"I mean I agree with your mother. You've been too stressed lately. You need to rest. This is the best place for you to relax."

"Oh, this is insane. I'm fine."

"Uh-huh. That's why you fainted in the E.R.," he said, his gaze holding hers in silent challenge.

It was hard to argue his point, she thought, sighing. Just as it had been hard for her to fight her attraction to him from the day she'd met him.

"Come on, let's get you something to eat," he said, pushing aside a stray strand of her hair. "An empty stomach is an invitation to faint again."

Her pulse raced at his fleeting touch, making her feel lightheaded. Heaven help her, she couldn't pass out again. "Maybe some toast," she conceded.

"That's all? You can have anything you want. Steak, chicken," he said, guiding her toward the door.

The thought of a heavy meal made her feel queasy. "Just toast, please. I can fix it myself."

"No," he said. "Anna's been waiting to fix something for you since you walked in the door. She said you looked terribly pale."

"There's no need to fuss," she said as she walked down the hallway beside him. She'd been too upset to notice much about Brock's house. Now that she was more composed, she took in the décor. Beautiful antiques stood on top of luxurious rugs. Heavy draperies lined the windows. Brass framed mirrors reflected over-the-top chandeliers.

"This is amazing. It must be like living in a palace," she said. "The antiques are—"

"—my mother's," he said with an edge of weariness in his voice. "As you know, I don't stay here very often. I feel more at ease in the apartment at the office."

"Oh," she said. "It's beautiful, but I can see why it might be hard to relax here. I'd be afraid I'd bump into something and break a million-dollar lamp."

He chuckled. "That would be one way to clear out some of this junk. Anna," he said as the housekeeper approached them. "Miss Linton says she would like toast."

Anna nodded, trying to hide her disapproval. "With beef tips, or turkey and mashed potatoes? Or perhaps crab?"

Elle shook her head. "Just butter and maybe jelly on the side."

Anna sighed. "If you're certain, Miss Linton. Would you like some wine?"

"Orange juice with ice and water," Elle said.

Anna nodded again. "I'll have it for you in the dining room in just a couple moments."

After Anna left, Elle turned to Brock. "I'm not really going to eat toast in a formal dining room, am I?"

He chuckled. "There's a breakfast table in the sun-room."

"Sounds wonderful," she said and followed him into a sunroom with a skylight that revealed the stars of the San Francisco night sky. Blinds were at perfect half-mast to showcase a courtyard with trees draped in white lights. She sank onto an overstuffed chair next to a glass table with a fresh flower arrangement. She looked around the room and breathed a sigh of relief. "I like this room."

"My father did, too," Brock said, sitting beside her. "He liked this room best. Got up before sunrise and read two newspapers here before going into work every day. Carol wanted to redecorate, but I refused. She has changed several rooms in the house, but not this one."

"Why do you call your mother Carol?" she asked.

"That's her name," he said.

"Still, most men call the woman who gave birth to them 'Mother' or 'Mom.'"

His gaze grew shuttered. "She's always been more Carol than Mother. Breeding was compulsory."

Elle gasped. "That's a terrible thing to say."

He glanced toward the entry. "Here comes your toast. Thanks, Anna."

Elle also thanked Anna and began to nibble the hot buttered bread. Anna had brought several different kinds. Any other time, she would have chosen wheat. Today she went straight for the sourdough. South Beach diet be damned. All she'd wanted since getting pregnant were carbs, carbs and more carbs. Thank goodness for prenatal vitamins.

Feeling Brock's gaze on her, she took a sip of orange juice. Something about him made her nervous in an exciting, forbidden way. Still. Even after that terrible scene this morning. She glanced away, frowning to herself.

"Jelly?" he asked.

She shook her head and took another bite of toast. "This is perfect."

His mouth lifted in a half-grin. Just as quickly, his smile fell. "How long have you known you were pregnant?"

Her throat closed around the bite of toast and she coughed, trying to swallow. She took another sip of juice. "Well, I haven't been regular lately."

"You didn't answer my question," he said.

She gnawed on her upper lip with her bottom teeth. "I suspected about six weeks ago."

His eyebrows shot up. "Six weeks?"

"I've been nauseous since then. At first, I thought it might be an intestinal virus." She shrugged. "Or stress. I avoided taking a home pregnancy test, but I made sure I was taking good vitamins. I was in denial," she confessed. She just couldn't believe she'd gotten pregnant by Brock, and she sure as heck had no clue what to do once her pregnancy was verified.

"So, how far along?" he asked.

"Three and a half months," she said. "I saw the doctor two weeks ago. He said the nausea should pass soon. I'm still waiting," she said, rolling her eyes.

"Why didn't you tell me?"

"I couldn't figure out how. I kept rehearsing all these different ways and none of them seemed right." Her stomach clenched and she dropped her piece of toast onto her plate. "I've had enough."

"You've hardly eaten anything," he said.

She shook her head. "I'm not hungry."

"But what about your health? What about the baby?" he demanded.

"I'm doing the best I can, and I'm taking prenatal vitamins. I have to believe that babies born with less food than I'm consuming have turned out fine, so I hope mine will, too." She pushed the plate away and stood. "I should go home."

Brock got to his feet, looming over her. "No. Stay here tonight."

She shook her head, but he gently put his hands on either side of her face and pushed her hair behind her ears. "You need rest. When you wake up in the morning, you'll feel better. Trust me."

Elle looked into his eyes and felt her heart twist and tug with opposing feelings. She trusted him, but at the same time, she didn't. She'd spent the last several months watching this man eat his competitors alive during the day and making her melt in his arms at night. He was passionate about the company. She'd never believed he could be equally passionate about her, yet when they'd been together, both of them had seemed to combust every time. She'd tried to tell herself it was just physical, but she'd known she was lying. She was falling for Brock. She *had* fallen for Brock.

Even though she'd slept for over five hours, she still felt exhausted. She couldn't fight her weariness and Brock at the same time. "Okay, but I'm leaving in the morning."

His gaze flickered with something indiscernible and she wished she could read him. She knew he could be a dangerous man.

"You're wise to give yourself a break, Elle. Let me walk you back to your room."

With his hand at her waist, she couldn't help breathing

a sigh of relief. It was temporary, the same way their relationship had been. Still, he'd been a respite for her as she had been for him. It was a shame the whole thing had blown up in their faces, but she'd always known there'd never been any other possible ending for their relationship.

Brock opened the door to the blue bedroom. "Anna refilled your water. Call if you need anything. Sweet sleep," he said and brushed his lips over her forehead.

Elle awakened the following morning when a sliver of the sun peeked through the curtains in the room. She savored the perfect cushiony firmness of the mattress and the cuddly cotton sheets. Even the pillow offered her head the perfect elevation. She sighed in contentment, inhaling the faintest whiff of eucalyptus and lavender.

Easing into consciousness, she thought about her mother. She should check on her. Three seconds passed and she thought of her grandfather. Frowning, she opened her eyes and realization hit her. She needed to check on him, too.

Sitting up, she remembered she was in Brock's Nob Hill home, and she definitely should be leaving. Sliding from the bed, she felt the padded carpet beneath her feet and rushed to the bathroom to shower and get on her way. By the end of bathing, though, she was fighting nausea.

Crap.

Taking deep, even breaths, she pulled on her clothes and walked down the hallway. She followed the sound of voices and found two people talking in the kitchen. "Good morning," she said.

Anna and a man she hadn't met yet turned to look at her. "Miss Linton?" Anna said. "May I get you some breakfast? Eggs, potatoes, bacon?"

Elle felt another roll of nausea. "Herbal tea and toast, please. Can you tell me where Mr. Maddox is?"

The woman smiled. "The sunroom. He likes to read the paper there in the morning when he's here," she said. "Would you like me to bring your toast and tea into the sunroom?"

"Yes, thank you very much," she replied.

As Anna had said, Brock sat in a chair in the sunroom, reading a newspaper. She felt a sudden attack of shyness. She'd stayed over at Brock's apartment at the company several times, but he'd never brought her here. Seeing him in the home he'd grown up in pointed out the differences between them. He was wealthy—and legitimate. She wasn't.

Silly, she told herself. She just needed to go home. "Brock," she said.

He immediately turned around and looked at her with those blazing blue eyes. "Good morning. Did you rest well?"

"Yes," she said. "I should go back home."

"How's your stomach feeling?" he asked.

"It's felt worse," she hedged.

"How's the morning sickness?"

She swallowed. "I'll be okay."

"Why don't you sit down and stop pushing yourself?"

"I have things to do," she said.

He pulled a sheet of paper from the table and handed it to her. "Here. Maybe this will help you take a break."

She glanced at the press release. It announced the engagement and subsequent wedding of Elle Linton and Brock Maddox.

Elle sank into a chair. "You haven't sent this out, have you?"

"It went out last night," he said.

She sucked in a deep breath and fought light-headedness. "Why?"

His gaze met hers. "You know it's the right thing. Do you really want to raise an illegitimate child? Doesn't your child deserve more?"

She closed her eyes, inhaling deeply, her heart torn. "We're not marrying for the right reasons."

"What could be a better reason than our child?" He frowned. "You look pale. Do you need water?"

She shook her head. "I feel sick," she said and raced for the bathroom by her room.

After her stomach calmed down, Elle wiped her face with a cool washcloth and brushed her teeth. Then she sank into a chair in the blue bedroom where she'd slept last night. She was trying to calm down but her mind was racing. *Marriage to Brock Maddox?* She shook her head at the possibility. At the same time she wondered how she could get out of it now that he'd released the news to the press. What choice did she have?

Hearing a tap at the door, she felt her heart race.

"Elle," Brock said. "Are you okay?"

Not really, she thought, but rose from the bed and opened the door. He looked down at her in concern. "If you're getting sick this often, you should see a doctor," he said.

"Well, you have to admit it's been a rough twenty-four

hours for me." She gazed at him, hard. "Why did you go ahead and announce our marriage when I'd already told you no?"

"Because I'm thinking of our child. Our child deserves the best I can give him or her, and I believe a real man doesn't shirk his responsibilities."

Like her father had. Elle had to admit she had never wanted the cloak of shame for her child that she had worn for most of her life. How many times had she been asked about her father and been forced to reply that she didn't have one? "This is too fast."

Brock's jaw tightened. "It can't happen fast enough, as far as I'm concerned," he said. "When news of your pregnancy hits, I want you wearing a wedding band and living in my home."

She frowned, feeling her stomach turn. "Is this all about image?"

"No," Brock said. "It's about doing the right thing for everyone concerned. I want you and our baby protected." He sighed. "You're right. This is fast, but it's necessary. If you were dreaming of a big church wedding, that's going to be difficult to pull off."

"I never pictured a big, fussy wedding for myself. Whenever I thought about it—and it wasn't often—I always thought a small beach wedding would be beautiful," she said. "But that wouldn't work now, so—"

"Yes, it can," he said, meeting her gaze. "I can make that happen. Would you like a new dress, and flowers?"

"No, it's not necessary," she demurred, looking away, feeling confused by his consideration.

"Let's schedule this for a week from now. Ask

someone you trust to go dress shopping with you, and choose some flowers. You can put it on my card."

"No, I—"

"I insist," he said, taking her hand.

Compelled by his tone, she met his gaze again.

"We're making a big commitment, Elle. It may not be what we'd planned, but it's going to work out. There's no reason for you to be miserable during the process."

But what about him? she wondered. He may be pushing forward on marrying her, but what were his real feelings? Especially since he knew she'd betrayed him for her grandfather. He still didn't know about her mother's treatments, and she found herself reluctant to tell him. Would he think it was just an excuse? Would he think she had tried to extract information from him in bed when in truth, falling for Brock and going to bed with him had *never* been part of the plan?

"How can we possibly make this work? With my family background and yours?" she asked.

"You and I will make it work," he said. "We have good motivation."

"But what about how I leaked company secrets?" she asked.

"That's in the past," he said firmly, his jaw locked. "We need to take care of the present and look toward the future."

Elle heard his words but his hard expression made her wonder if he would ever be able to truly forgive her.

Exiting the elevator in the Powell Street office of Maddox Communications on Monday, Brock felt a sense of responsibility hit him, as it often did. It was hard to believe, but even the seven-story Beaux Arts building built in 1910 would have been demolished by the wrecking ball if not for his father's determination to restore it. These days, the reception area looked totally different than it had during James's heyday. Continuing his father's tradition of embracing modern technology, Brock had arranged for two seventy-inch plasma screens to sit on either side of the reception desk, showing videos and commercials produced by Maddox Communications.

Nodding to the receptionist, Brock walked down the hallway, noting Elle's empty desk outside his office. He hadn't needed to fire her or ask her to resign. She'd known she wouldn't be welcome in the office any longer. He felt a twinge of longing followed quickly by a blast of impatience with himself. From the first day she'd begun working for him, Elle had inspired a strange combination of emotions inside him.

If he'd been smarter, perhaps he wouldn't have allowed himself to get involved with her so easily. But she was smart and warm, and her sultry blue eyes had distracted him after his fiancée had left him wondering if he should even try to get involved in a serious relationship with a woman. When they'd given in to their impulses, she hadn't asked him for more. That had only made him ravenous for her.

His need could have brought down the agency his father had worked so hard to build. How could Elle have tricked him like that? How could she have lied with her kisses and passion?

He thought of her grandfather and wondered if he would have done the same for his father if he'd been asked. Brock already knew the answer. He would have done anything his father asked because he'd provided Brock with unswerving love and loyalty.

Pushing aside his mixed emotions, he walked into the office that had belonged to James Maddox. Brock had changed it very little since his father's death. Somehow, keeping the same furniture made him feel as if his father were still nearby. The founder of Maddox Communications, however, would be turning in his grave if he knew Brock had gotten sexually involved with his assistant, let alone the granddaughter of Athos Koteas.

He called the human resources director to send up a temporary assistant. Someone trustworthy, he emphasized, feeling a surge of bitterness and tamping it down. Stabbing his fingers through his hair, he took some time to prioritize the work on his desk. Brock was still babying the deal with The Prentice Group. Marrying Elle would dispel any objections the conservative client would have about Brock's involvement with a coworker.

He swore under his breath. This week had been a nightmare. Finding out that Elle had betrayed him had been bad enough, but learning of her pregnancy had totally turned his head around. Even though he wasn't sure he could ever trust her again, seeing her in his house had done something to him. Having her there had made the house feel more like a home to him.

Brock had lost his fiancée because he'd ignored his personal life in order to focus on the company. Although he wasn't in love with Elle, he did have feelings for her.

Add that to the fact that she was carrying his child, and he was determined to make their relationship legal.

His BlackBerry rang and he checked the incoming number. His brother, Flynn. He'd probably gotten wind of the press release. Brock picked up. "Brock here."

"I suppose congratulations are in order," Flynn said. "This is sudden."

Brock felt a twist of discomfort. Since Flynn had gotten married and stepped down as VP at the firm, Brock had found himself wanting more camaraderie with his brother. "You know me. When I make a decision, I move fast."

"I'll say. Are you headed to the courthouse tomorrow?"

"We're getting married next week," Brock said. "It'll be a beach ceremony. I'd like you to come."

Silence followed. "Thanks. I'm honored."

"I'll give you the details later. How is Renee?" Brock asked, referring to Flynn's wife.

"Happily bearing my child," Flynn said. Brock could hear the contentment in his brother's voice—for once, he felt a sliver of envy. He couldn't honestly say that Elle was happy to be pregnant with his child.

"She's excited about attending the shower for Jason and Lauren Reagert's baby this weekend."

Brock nodded. It seemed pregnancy was in the water at his firm lately. Jason was a huge new talent at Maddox, and when he'd married his wife, Lauren, he'd done so to avoid a scandal. It hadn't taken long for Jason and Lauren to fall in love. Brock didn't expect the same for himself, but he was determined to make his marriage to Elle successful, at least.

"I'm glad things worked out for them," Brock said.

"Any chance your marriage will make you leave the office on time once in a while?"

Brock gave a cynical laugh. "On time? There's no such thing as a regular quitting time in my life until I'm sure Golden Gate can't do any more damage to Maddox." Even now, he wasn't sure exactly how much Elle had told Koteas, and he refused to grill her in her current state.

"Okay, bro, just don't forget to live your life. See you next week," Flynn said.

"Next week. Bye." Brock disconnected the call. He glanced out the window of his office at the shoppers and trolley cars in constant movement. He remembered the words his father once said when he'd been daydreaming instead of completing a school assignment: *The world won't stop just because you've got problems.*

So true, he thought, pulling himself out of his distracted state. He picked up the phone to call a jeweler.

Three

Elle spent the day visiting her mother at home and her grandfather at the hospital. When she'd broken the news to her mother that she was going to marry Brock after all, her mother had been ecstatic. Elle still couldn't believe it. The very thought of it locked up her brain, so she'd put off shopping for a dress or anything else. When Brock had called to invite her to dinner at his house, her mother had insisted she join him.

A chauffer picked her up at the condo and took her to Brock's at six o'clock, but he wasn't home yet. She wasn't surprised. She'd worked for him long enough to know his first, second and third loves were Maddox Communications. He was the most dynamic, complex man she'd ever met and despite every reason she'd had to not get involved with him, she couldn't stop herself.

At the time that she'd fallen for Brock, she'd just been glad to get a piece of him.

Now, everything was a mess.

She sat in the den, which was far too fussy for her taste, and sipped a glass of orange juice and sparkling water. Tired from the day, she sighed, slipped off her shoes and closed her eyes. It seemed like seconds passed and then Brock was standing in front of her.

He studied her with a cryptic grin hovering on his lips. "I should have known you were pregnant when I had to wake you up to go home after we made love all those nights."

Feeling her cheeks heat at memories of their intimacy, she straightened and pushed her feet into her shoes. "I have to be honest. For a while there, I was worried that something more serious might have been wrong with me."

"But you've been thoroughly checked out?"

She nodded. "The doctor told me it's not unusual to have a lack of energy. Supposedly that changes sometime during the second trimester."

"Good," he said and extended his hand. "Let's have dinner. Then I have a surprise for you."

"A surprise?" she echoed, feeling a secret rush of pleasure followed quickly by caution. "Is this a good surprise or a bad surprise?" she asked as he led her into the sunroom.

"I think most women would call it a good surprise," he said. "Don't ask any more questions. You'll know soon enough."

During dinner, he only made vague references to his work. Elle felt a stab of loss over his previous openness with her. She'd never realized how much she appreciated the way he'd shared his thoughts and concerns about the company. Of course, she couldn't blame him for being guarded since he'd learned she'd been spying on him. Still, the loss tugged at her. They would never be the same again. He changed the subject and asked her about her activities.

"You visited both your mother and your grandfather? I told you to rest."

"If I'd rested any longer, I would have screamed," she told him. "Can you tell me you would be happy to lie in bed all day long?"

A flicker of heat shot through his gaze. "Under the right circumstances," he said.

She felt a surprising sliver of arousal but shook it off. Even during their affair, they'd rarely stayed in bed more than an hour or two. "I would like to see those circumstances," she said.

The housekeeper poked her head inside the room. "Mr. Walthall is here, Mr. Maddox. He's waiting in the front living room when you're ready."

"Ah, the surprise," he said and glanced at her plate. "Are you sure you've had enough to eat?"

"Plenty," she said. "I was told to try to stick with small, frequent meals."

"Then we'll make sure that's what you get. I'll tell Anna." He stood. "Ready?"

"Brock, it's not your housekeeper's job to make sure I'm eating properly."

"She'll love it. My mother is on the twig-and-berry diet, so Anna will be thrilled at the prospect of fattening you up."

She shot him a dark look. "I don't plan to get fat. I just plan to be healthy."

He shrugged. "That's what I said."

Not really, she thought, but didn't say so as they turned the corner into the formal living room where a man sat with several large cases. He stood and extended his hand. "Mr. Maddox. Phillip Walthall. I'm happy we can be of service to you. And this is?" he asked, looking at Elle.

"This is my fiancée, Elle Linton," Brock said. "Elle, Mr. Walthall is a jeweler. He's going to show you some selections so you can choose something you'd like."

"An engagement ring," she said, unable to keep the dismay from her voice. She was still trying to pretend this wasn't going to happen. How in the world would she be able to avoid it if she were wearing a ring all the time? "I don't need one."

"Of course you do."

Mr. Walthall laughed. "Give me a chance to change your mind."

Brock urged her to sit while the jeweler pulled out a tray of diamonds that made her blink. Although she and her mother had lived in a nice place, they'd been careful with their money. Her mother had always worked and Elle had attended a state college. She'd never envisioned wearing a ring that looked like it cost more than her tuition had. "These are all so big," she said.

Mr. Walthall chuckled again. "That's not a complaint, is it?"

"I'm just overwhelmed," she said.

"What I like to ask my clients is, what is your dream engagement ring? All these years, you must have secretly dreamed about the ring you might receive from the man you chose to marry," Mr. Walthall said.

Elle closed her eyes and took a deep breath. Had she ever dreamed about an engagement ring? More often, she'd dreamed of having a father. Then, she'd dreamed of finding a man who would love her as much as she loved him. She'd known Brock would never love her like that, but she hadn't been able to resist him. If she was going to have a ring, why not make it meaningful, at least to her? "What is December's birthstone?"

Mr. Walthall lifted his shoulders. "It depends. Blue topaz, tanzanite or ruby, depending on your point of view."

"Why do you ask?" Brock asked.

"The baby is due in December," she said.

She saw sadness and something else she couldn't quite read in his eyes. "My father's birthday is in December."

Elle felt a riveting connection with Brock ripple through her. How amazing that their child would be born in the same month as Brock's father. "I'd like to see some options that would include blue topaz, tanzanite or ruby."

"Very nice. I always like it when a couple makes a choice that has personal meaning," Mr. Walthall said.

Within a matter of minutes, she had chosen a series of beautiful tanzanite stones to accent a solitaire diamond. "A half-carat diamond," she suggested.

Mr. Walthall's face fell. "A half?"

"Eight carats," Brock corrected.

Elle felt her eyes nearly bug out of her face. "I'll need a crane," she protested.

"You may not realize this, but your ring is not just a reflection of your taste. It's a reflection of me, too," Brock said.

She bit her lip, thinking he was spending an obscene amount of money. "You could feed a third-world country with this," she wailed.

"If it will make it easier for you, I'll send out a donation matching the cost of the ring tomorrow," Brock said wryly.

"Can we knock it down to three?" she asked.

"Five. That's final," he said.

Elle looked at the jeweler, who appeared totally bemused by their negotiations. "I guess it's five."

Mr. Walthall nodded. "It will be a beautiful ring."

"When can you have it?" Brock asked.

"When would you like it?" Mr. Walthall replied.

"Tomorrow," he said.

"As you wish, sir." Mr. Walthall put the trays into his suitcase and clicked them closed. "It's a pleasure to do business with you. If you change your mind and wish to increase the size of the diamond tomorrow morning, just give me a call and we can make the adjustment."

The jeweler left and silence fell over Brock and Elle like a blanket.

Brock cleared his throat. "I didn't realize the baby would be born the same month as my father's birthday."

She looked up at him. "Does it bother you?"

He paused a long moment and his gaze softened. "No. It sounds crazy, but I think it will be a comfort."

She stared at him in surprise. He was a strong man who never asked for comfort, who never seemed to need comfort. Unable to keep herself from reaching out to him, she lifted her hand.

He drew back. "I want you to stay here tonight," he said.

"Why?" she demanded, hurt by his rejection of her gesture. "There's no reason I can't stay with my mother until—" She stopped. "Until we're married."

His face turned to stone. "You're still doing too much. I can be sure you'll be taken care of if you're here."

Elle sighed. She considered arguing, but the truth was she was tired. It wasn't as if she would be sharing Brock's bed. The thought made her stomach clench and her skin burn. What would happen when they made love again? Would it be like before? Was it possible that they could share the passion they once had?

She forced herself to focus on the baby. "I do need the rest," she said. "But I want to stay at my mother's tomorrow night."

"I'll send a driver and mover to pack your things and bring them here," he said and looked at her with a possessive gaze. "Plan to stay here tomorrow night. The ring will be ready, and I'll want to put it on your finger."

By Saturday, Elle still wasn't accustomed to the weight of the engagement ring on her finger. She was thankful for the distraction of the baby shower for Jason and Lauren. One of Lauren's neighbors in Mission Hill was holding the party at her house. Brock had insisted that his chauffeur take her there. He didn't want her driving, which she thought was ridiculous.

She carried her gift for Jason and Lauren's baby boy

into the house. Blue balloons and decorations filled the foyer and the large living room had been made ready for the baby shower.

Lauren, with a big baby bump, glanced up as Elle walked into the room. "Elle," she said, rising to her feet. "I'm so glad you could come. Look at that gorgeous gift. Tell me what's in it," she said, beaming with pregnant radiance.

Elle couldn't help smiling. "You'll have to open it," she said.

Lauren made a face. "You can't give me a hint?"

"It's blue," Elle said.

Lauren laughed. "Come here and have some wine," she said. "I can't drink it but the rest of you can. I want to toast your engagement." She put her arm around Elle and guided her to a table. "How did you keep it so quiet?"

Elle bit her lip. "It just kind of happened. I don't think either of us expected it. Hey, that punch looks delicious."

"That's for me," Lauren said, "since I'm on no booze. But you can have some." Lauren poured a ladle full in one punch cup and then another. She lifted hers in a toast. "Wishing you the happiest, most wonderful marriage ever."

Elle felt her throat knot with emotion. *How could this marriage possibly be the happiest ever?* "Thank you," she said and took the teensiest sip possible. The last thing she wanted to do was get sick at the shower.

"Give me the scoop," Lauren said. "From the press release, it sounded like you two will be married soon. What's the rush?"

Elle felt her stomach turn. "You know Brock. When he makes a decision, he moves fast."

Lauren laughed. "You're so right."

Elle felt the rise of nausea in the back of her throat. "Excuse me. I need to use the powder room. Could you tell me where it is?"

"Oh, right through that hallway," Lauren said and pointed. "Go right ahead. I'll be here when you get back."

Elle rushed to the powder room. After she recovered, she splashed her face with water and rinsed out her mouth. Taking a deep breath, she tried to calm herself. She walked outside and immediately ran into Lauren, who studied her with concern. "Come here for a moment," she said and whisked her away to a private bedroom. "Are you okay?"

"Of course," Elle said. "I just feel a little off. It's probably a little virus or something I ate."

Lauren paused and shook her head. "You're pregnant, aren't you?"

Elle's heart leaped into her throat. She would have tried to lie but the sympathy in Lauren's eyes prevented her. "Please don't tell anyone. Brock insisted that we get married."

Lauren nodded. "I've been in your same situation."

"I'm not sure it's exactly the same," Elle muttered, thinking of her grandfather and how she had betrayed Brock.

"Close enough," Lauren said. "Just try to be open to possibilities. It could turn out much differently than you expect—I speak from experience. Most importantly, take care of yourself. You've got someone precious growing inside you."

Elle felt a sudden urge to cry. Her eyes burned with unshed tears. "Thank you," she said. "You don't know how much I appreciate that."

Lauren pulled her into an embrace. "Have you thought about names?"

"That's way in the future," Elle said. "I'm still just getting through today."

"The good times will come soon. Believe me," Lauren said.

Elle could only hope her friend was right.

Two days later, Elle put on the dress she and her mother had found on sale at an exclusive shop not far from Maddox Communications. Elle had thought about visiting Brock at the office at the time, then quickly dismissed the idea. He wouldn't have wanted her there.

"You look beautiful," her mother said, hugging her. "I'm so happy you're getting married. I'm so happy your baby will have the father you never had. You have no idea what a relief that is, Elle." Her mother sighed. "I wish I could have given you that."

Elle's heart twisted. "You gave me the best things in the world. You, attention and bubbles."

Her mother laughed. "You always did like bubbles." She put her hands on Elle's belly. "I bet your baby will like bubbles, too."

"You and I both will blow bubbles for him or her," Elle said, unable to resist a smile.

"Yes, we will," her mother said. "But first, it's time for

you to get married." She leaned toward Elle and brushed a kiss over her cheek. "You're beautiful, sweetheart. Your Brock is so lucky. Be happy, my girl. Be happy."

Elle could only hope. She forced her lips into a smile as her stomach turned somersaults. She looked in the mirror. Was that really her? That woman wearing ivory with baby's breath in her hair? Was she really going to marry Brock Maddox? And could they really make their marriage work?

She and her mother rode in a chauffeured car to the beach location for the wedding. The sun had burned off most of the morning fog, so at least there would be no rain. The car pulled to a stop in front of the private cottage where they would eat a meal afterward. Elle spotted Brock in the distance. Her heart stuttered at the sight of him. When she'd first met him, she'd never dared to dream they would be married. There were too many obstacles. She wondered again if this was a mistake.

"Elle," her mother said, lifting her hand to smooth the crease between Elle's brows. "Stop worrying. This is a happy day."

"But—" Elle said, fear twisting her inside like a vise.

"No buts," her mother said. "Remember. Never trouble trouble unless trouble troubles you."

Elle smiled at the saying her mother had quoted to her so many times throughout the years. She took a deep breath. Just for today, she would try not to trouble trouble. She followed her mother from the car to the cottage where the hostess greeted them.

"Everyone is ready for you," the woman said. "Especially the groom. The harpist is already playing."

"Harpist?" Elle said in surprise, craning to look out the window.

"Oh, I'm sorry," the hostess said. "Perhaps that was supposed to be a surprise."

Her mother's eyes danced with excitement. "I'll go first, like we planned," she said, smoothing her blue dress then lifting her hand to Elle's cheek. "I'm so happy for you, and for the baby."

Elle's stomach dipped. "I love you, Mom," she said.

Elle watched her mother walk down the stone path, then down smooth wooden planks over the sandy beach. The blue-gray Pacific rippled with white crests. Gathering her courage, she walked toward the door. A bouquet was pushed into her hands.

Blinking, Elle glanced at the hostess again in surprise.

The hostess smiled. "Mr. Maddox insisted. They're beautiful, aren't they?"

Elle looked down at the arrangement of white lilies and blood-red roses, and couldn't help thinking of all the bad blood that had flowed between her family and Brock's. Could their marriage sew together the jagged, bitter edges of competition?

Closing her eyes, she took a deep breath. One step at a time. The hostess opened the door and Elle stepped outside.

Brock watched as the door to the cottage opened and Elle appeared. The wind lifted tendrils of her hair and the hem of her lacy dress fluttered against her shapely upper calves. She had an ethereal look to her, almost angelic, but he knew different in every way. She'd been a sensual goddess in his bed, fulfilling his every need. At work, she had seemed like the perfect assistant, but the truth was she'd been tricking him every day, deceiving him.

He felt a stab of bitterness in his throat and swallowed it. There were more important things, he reminded himself. The baby. *His* baby. If there was anything his father had taught him, it was duty to the company and duty to his family.

His mother had been a dutiful but passionless wife and mother. Brock knew Elle would be different. He'd already experienced her passion and he knew, deep down in his bones, that she would love their child. Their child wouldn't be regarded as an obligation. Elle would receive their child as a precious gift and responsibility. As for their relationship, they would work that out along the way.

She met his gaze and though he couldn't see her eyes from where he stood, he guessed they were probably turbulent with conflicting emotions. She looked like a prized princess, her head held high, walking tall, only the smallest bump showing when the wind flattened her dress against her abdomen.

Brock couldn't tear his gaze from her. She'd been the lover who'd both comforted him and turned him upside down. And betrayed him.

Despite that last fact, he still craved her. He should have hated himself for it, but he knew that once she bore his name, he would be her first priority. There would be no more division of loyalties. Her loyalty would be to him.

She took the last few steps and stood next to him, searching his gaze. Just as he'd anticipated, her eyes were full of emotion. He took her hand in his and watched her inhale quickly. It gave him pleasure to know that he still got past her reserve.

He lifted her hand to his lips and kissed it, all the while looking into her eyes. "We're ready," he said in a low voice to the officiant, and the ceremony began. He repeated the vows he'd never made before and watched as she did the same.

"I now pronounce you man and wife," the minister said. "You may kiss the bride."

The sun came out from behind a cloud and Brock pulled Elle into his arms. She felt both strong and delicate against him. He lowered his mouth to hers and gave her a kiss of promise. He felt her tremble. "It will be okay," he whispered against her ear.

"It will," she whispered, but didn't look at all convinced.

Elle felt numb. The steak dinner arranged for her wedding celebration may as well have been sawdust in her mouth. Her hands were freezing, but she forced herself to nod and smile at Flynn and his wife, Renee.

"You look beautiful," Renee said.

"Thank you," Elle replied, feeling a stab of guilt for betraying the woman by using their friendship to get more secrets for her grandfather to use against Maddox. Renee had been a friend to her. She was surprised Renee was willing to speak to her, let alone extend her good wishes.

"I can't tell you how glad I am to see my brother get married," Flynn said. "He's been married to the company for so long, I was starting to wonder…"

"No need to wonder anymore," Brock said, lifting his glass of wine. "Thanks for being here," he said to Flynn. Then he turned to Elle. "To my wife—may our love grow, our commitment deepen and our joy overflow."

"I can only hope," Elle whispered under her breath, lifting her glass of sparkling water. The passion she glimpsed in his laser-blue eyes reminded her why she'd fallen for Brock. His passion for work, for life and, in the dark of night in his office apartment, for her.

Her mother and Brock's brother and sister-in-law clapped in approval.

"Honeymoon plans?" Flynn asked.

In one heartbeat, Brock's eyes turned to ice. He looked away. "Later," he said. "I have to dig the company out of its current crisis."

Elle felt her stomach sink to her knees and was glad she was sitting down. She knew she was the reason for the "current crisis."

An hour later, after their guests had departed, Elle left the cottage in Brock's limo. It was so silent she could barely breathe.

"You look beautiful," Brock said, but didn't meet her gaze.

She tried without success to take a deep breath. This was a huge mistake, she thought. Was there any way she could go back? Was an annulment possible? "Thank you," she said in a quiet voice. "The flowers and harp were very nice."

He nodded. "Every woman deserves something special at her wedding."

"Who told you that?"

He paused. "Renee."

"That was generous of her."

"I thought so," he said.

She bit her lip. "I don't blame everyone for being angry with me, and I don't blame you for resenting me—"

"I don't," he cut in. "Your loyalty was with your grandfather. Now it's with me."

It was so much more complicated than that, she thought. As the limo pulled up in front of Brock's grand home, he got out of the car and escorted Elle through the front door. His combination of good manners and primal strength had captivated her from the beginning. He could appear so smooth and civilized, but if necessary, he had the instincts of a street fighter and would go for the jugular to protect what was his.

She wondered how far his possessiveness toward her extended. Was it just for the baby?

The housekeeper approached them with a beaming smile. "Congratulations, both of you. I'm so happy for you. And you just look lovely, Miss Linton." She covered her mouth. "Oh, I should have said Mrs. Maddox."

Elle's heart skipped at the sound of her new name. Pushing aside her conflicting feelings, she took the woman's hands in hers. "Thank you, Anna. You're very kind."

"Please have Roger move Elle's things into my suite," Brock said.

"Right away. We'll have it done in no time," the housekeeper said and walked down the hallway.

Elle struggled with a surge of panic. "Your suite," she echoed, meeting his gaze.

"My suite has two bedrooms, two baths, a study, den and small exercise room. At some point my mother will return here, hopefully for a brief period," he said in a dry voice. "The less she knows about my private life, the better—she's been known to cause trouble. There won't be as many questions if you're living in my suite. Now, I need to go back to the office, but I'll be home later tonight. Roger will be on hand for you to move the rest of your things here during the next few days, but I don't want you to overdo it. You've had a busy day."

He looked deep into her eyes and she saw a glimpse of the passion they'd shared. But just as quickly, the fire was gone. "I'll see you later," he said, leaving her alone on their wedding night.

Most of Maddox's employees had left by the time Brock invited Logan Emerson into his office after hours. He'd hired the private investigator a short while back when it had become clear that someone was leaking company secrets. Brock's gut sank again as he remembered the exact moment he'd learned Elle had been the one. Elle, his uncorrupted island, had been twisting the knife at the same time she'd made love to him.

Logan sat across from Brock. "I just heard about your marriage. I was surprised."

"She's pregnant with my child," Brock said.

Logan, usually reserved, gave a low whistle of surprise. "I'm assuming that means you won't be prosecuting her."

"You assume correctly," Brock said.

"I understand. Well, it appears as if my job here is done," Logan said.

Brock frowned. "Perhaps not. Maddox is still at a critical point. There are several possibilities I want to explore. Quickly, of course. I'd like to keep you on longer until we see how things shake out."

"No problem," he said. "Just let me know what you need."

"Good," Brock said and stood. "That's all for now."

Logan extended his hand. "Best wishes on your marriage. It's not my place to say, really, but I don't believe Elle enjoyed the deception."

Brock just nodded. He was still coming to grips with how his life had been turned upside down in such a short time. "Thank you."

Brock reviewed his plans for the rest of the week, but it took longer than usual because he kept thinking about Elle's deception. He clenched his hands, then released them. The only thing that helped him was the fact that he would have done the same for his father. And he'd do anything for the sake of the company. It was his duty, his destiny, his heritage.

Hours later, after he left work, he climbed the stairs to his suite. He noticed one of the bedroom doors was closed but the one to the master bedroom was left open. The lamp on his bedside table was on, and the covers on his king-size bed were turned back. Walking through the doorway, he studied the room, catching the whiff of a sweet scent. His gaze caught on a small, clear vase on the bedside table. Inside stood one ruby-red rose. From Elle's bouquet. He saw a piece of paper sitting next to the vase.

Thank you. Elle.

It wasn't the first time she'd thanked him for giving her flowers, but still, he was touched. The rose reminded him of the passion they'd shared before everything had come to light. He lifted it and inhaled the fragrance, wondering if they would ever feel that sweetness they'd shared again.

Four

Elle set her alarm so she could join Brock for breakfast. She wasn't at all sure how to make their marriage work, but she knew that avoiding him wouldn't help. Shaking off her sleepiness, she beat him to the sunroom by a minute and a half.

His eyebrows lifted in surprise as he entered the room.

She felt a tiny surge of gratification and smiled. "Good morning." She lifted the hot pot of coffee. "Ready for your first cup?"

"Yes, thank you," he said, and she poured for him.

She felt his gaze skim over her as he took a sip. "Where's yours?"

She shook her head. "Coffee's not on my list these days."

"Why not?"

"Caffeine's a no-no during pregnancy," she said. "It helps that I've temporarily lost my taste for it."

Brock's eyebrows furrowed. "Ooh. That's tough. How does that affect your sleepiness?"

She laughed. "I'm still in the sleepy stage."

"Sleepy stage?"

"I want to take naps constantly. I've actually felt like this for several weeks and was hoping I wasn't coming down with something. But I guess in a way, I did. The nine-month flu," she said, chuckling to herself.

Brock smiled as he lifted his cup for another sip.

"The good news is any day now I'm supposed to start feeling a burst of energy and I'll be incredibly productive."

"As long as you don't plan on running a marathon," he said. "Your main job is to take care of yourself and the baby."

"At some point, I'll need to make some plans for a nursery," she ventured, watching his expression carefully.

He nodded and met her gaze. "Eventually, the child can be moved into his or her own room. My suite was originally designed for my wife and me to share the master bedroom, and the infant to sleep where you are currently."

Elle felt a jolt of heat as sensual memories flooded her mind. Did Brock want her in his bed again? What would be different between them? "Is that what you want?"

"We don't need to make that decision right now. You've been through a lot during the last couple of weeks. Make sure you don't do too much today when you're packing and unpacking your belongings. That's what Roger is for."

She nodded and a silence fell between them. How she longed for the easy conversation they'd once shared.

He glanced at his watch. "Time for me to go."

"So early?" The words popped out before she knew it.

"Breakfast meeting with—" He stopped as if he remembered he couldn't share that information with her. She'd shown him she couldn't be trusted. Elle hated that. She wondered if it would always be this way between them—oh-so-careful with edited information.

"Have a good day," she managed.

"You, too," he said and walked away.

Her stomach twisted and she forced herself to take a quick breath. *Give it time,* she told herself. *You haven't even been married twenty-four hours.*

Later that day, Elle's mother helped her pack. "This is the sad part," her mother said. "As happy as I am for you that you're married and moving to live with your husband, I'll miss you terribly."

Her mother's tone tugged at her heart and Elle gave her a hug. "It's not like I'm moving very far. We can see each other as often as we like. And you know you can call me for anything," Elle said firmly.

"I'm glad I finally joined that support group last year," Suzanne said. "We really do help take care of each other, and heaven knows I don't want to be a burden to you."

Elle held up her hand. "Stop that craziness. You know you're no burden. I just don't want you to push yourself too much, especially now that you've gone back to work part-time."

"Look who's talking," her mother said. "You're the one who's been working double time lately, preparing for the wedding and moving. Thank goodness Brock won't let you overdo any longer. I can tell he's a strong man."

"Yes, he is," Elle murmured, thinking Brock wouldn't let her within a mile of the office at this point.

"What I don't understand is why you didn't tell him about the baby as soon as you knew," her mother said, her brows knitting in a furrow.

"Aside from the fact that it was an office affair?" Elle said, even though it had been far more than that to her. She smiled and gave her mother another squeeze. "You know, things just get complicated sometimes."

Later that evening, Elle tried to help Roger carry a box upstairs but was brushed aside. He shot her an appalled glance. "Absolutely not, Mrs. Maddox. Mr. Maddox would have my head. I would have my head," the older man said.

"Okay, okay," Elle said, stepping aside. "At least let me get you something to drink."

Roger gave a heavy sigh. "Thank you."

Elle checked out the small refrigerator in the mini-kitchen and pulled out a bottle of water. She walked back to the smaller bedroom where Roger was stacking the last of the boxes.

"Now, you know not to lift these," he said, shooting her a warning gaze with iron-gray eyebrows over dark gray eyes.

"Maybe we should spread them out a little," she suggested.

He lifted his hand as she approached to help. "I'll do it, but only with the agreement that you leave a light on at night so you won't trip on your way to the bathroom."

"Excellent idea," she said, clapping her hands. "I see why Brock relies on you."

Roger's lips lifted in a half grin. "Thank you. I'm honored by the compliment."

A few moments later, she thrust the bottle of water into his hands and impulsively hugged the cranky man.

He gave a low chuckle of surprise. "Now, promise you won't try to do too much this evening. Rome wasn't built in a day, you know?"

During the next hour, Elle emptied four boxes into drawers and the generous walk-in closet. Glancing up, she noticed the late hour and decided to take a break with a hot shower. She wondered where Brock was. Was he staying at his office apartment tonight? In the bed they had shared so many times after work?

The notion twisted something inside her and she tried not to think about it as the water spilled over her. She tried to visualize the warmth washing away all her worries as she rubbed her belly. Elle couldn't overthink the future right now. Dealing with today was enough.

She dried off and pulled a comfy cotton nightshirt over her head. She combed through her wet hair and slid her arms into a long terry-cloth robe that tied at her waist. Her stomach growled, surprising her. It was late and she needed to sleep. What had she read recently about foods one should eat at bedtime? A banana. She'd seen a bunch downstairs. She would eat half of one, she decided, and headed for the stairs.

She took the first step, then the next. Her foot caught in the hem of her robe and she grabbed at the banister but she was too late. She fell headfirst down the stairs and felt the impact of the wooden steps against her chest and belly. A scream escaped her. She grabbed and clutched for anything to stop her. She screamed again.

Anna and Roger appeared at the bottom of the steps, their faces filled with horror.

Elle closed her eyes at their expressions. Oh, god, help her. The baby. The baby.

Roger rushed to her side. "Miss, are you okay? Are you awake?"

Elle took a deep breath, trying to take stock of her body. She felt sore in places she couldn't identify. "I'm conscious," she said, opening her eyes again. "But I'm afraid," she whispered. "I want to make sure the baby is okay."

Roger's eyebrows drew together. "We'll take you to the hospital immediately," he said.

Brock marched into the emergency room, his heart pounding against his chest. He stopped at the desk. "Brock Maddox. My wife is here," he said in a curt voice.

The receptionist nodded. "Please come this way," she said and led him down a hallway to a room. She opened the door and he spotted Elle reclining on a table with Anna and Roger by her side. The atmosphere in the room was grim.

All three of them looked at him.

"Mr. Maddox—" Roger and Anna said in unison.

Brock felt the twist in his gut tighten further. "Thank you for getting her here," he said, then turned his attention to Elle. "How are you?"

She bit her lip. "Waiting on the ultrasound," she said, her expression full of fear. "I wish I weren't so clumsy," she whispered, her eyes shiny with unshed tears.

Brock rushed to her side and took her hand in his. "I'll make sure you're okay," he said.

"But what about the baby?" she asked, her voice breaking.

Roger cleared his throat. "We'll be in the waiting room."

"I feel so horrible," Elle said. "What if my carelessness—"

He pressed his fingers over her lips. "You can't think that," he said.

A young woman dressed in white walked through the doorway. "Hello, I'm Dr. Shen." She extended her hand to Elle and then to Brock. "I understand Mom took a tumble. Babies are amazingly resilient, so your little one is likely okay. Let's check it out."

The doctor squirted some gel on Elle's belly and rubbed a device over her.

Brock watched as a jumble of a being appeared on the screen before them.

"Good, strong heartbeat right there," Dr. Shen said, pointing to the flicker on the screen. She moved the device. "Everything looks good so far. Placenta's intact."

She removed the device and handed it to the nurse,

then turned to Brock and Elle. "You might have some bruises tomorrow, but your baby is fine. Just be careful around stairs, okay?"

Elle gave a big nod of relief. "Very careful."

The doctor scrawled her signature on the notebook screen. "You're released. And we can give you a copy of the ultrasound video, if you'd like."

"Thank you," Elle said.

"Thanks," Brock echoed. Elle looked at his face, which was full of wonder and awe. She understood. The heartbeat, the movement of the tiny legs and arms—it was overwhelming. And amazing.

The nurse wiped the gel off of Elle's abdomen. "You can get dressed now," she said.

Elle took an audible breath. "Sorry to bother you with this," she murmured and moved to slide from the table.

Brock wrapped his arm around her shoulders. "You can't be serious."

Elle bit her lip. "I know you have other things to do."

"There's nothing more important," he said. "Nothing."

"It almost didn't seem real before," she said. "But it does now. We're going to have a baby."

He nodded and smiled. "Yes, we are."

Two days later, Elle couldn't stand her Brock-imposed exile from the outside world any longer. Now, she desperately needed to get out.

The housekeeper frowned as Elle put her hand on

the doorknob of the front door. "You're not going out, are you?" Anna said.

Elle turned to look at the caring woman. "Yes, I am. The doctor says it's fine. I haven't had any spotting. The ultrasound looked good. Some physical activity will be good for me."

"Mr. Maddox won't like it," she said.

"Yes, well, he would just as soon see me wrapped in a cocoon until my due date. That's not going to happen," Elle said firmly.

"I can't say I blame you, but you really did give us a scare. If Mr. Maddox should ask where you are, what should I tell him?"

Elle smiled. "Tell him I'm shopping for a shorter robe."

The housekeeper chuckled. "Good for you. Let me call Roger. He can drive you."

"Oh, that's not necessary at all," Elle protested.

The housekeeper shook her head. "Mr. Maddox would want you to go with a driver. It won't take but a moment."

Elle cooled her heels, then stepped into the town car and directed Roger to take her to an outlet.

"Outlet?" Roger echoed as if it were a foreign word. "Are you sure you wouldn't rather go downtown? That's where the senior Mrs. Maddox always goes."

"No, I love Nordstrom's Rack," she said, settling back in her seat.

Roger let her out at the front door and Elle walked into the busy store. She wandered through the lingerie section, admiring the silk gowns. She would be too large for them soon enough, she thought, sliding her hand over her belly. Finding a rack of robes, she flipped through the selection and pulled out a red one. "You'll look like a giant, mutant cherry," she muttered to herself.

Her cell phone rang and she saw Brock's number on her caller ID. Wincing, she answered. "Hello?"

"What are you doing at Nordstrom's Rack?"

"Buying a short robe," she said. "I assume your spies informed you?"

"Roger told me you insisted on going to an outlet," Brock said. "I can afford to get you a robe and anything else you need, for God's sake. You don't have to watch your pennies. And you sure as hell don't need to be shopping at outlets."

"But I like shopping in outlets. It's like hunting is for men. Bagging the one with the biggest rack in one shot."

Silence followed. "I've never heard it described that way."

"Well, I'm glad to know I've provided you with a new analogy," she said. "Maybe you can use it for a campaign."

"Hmm. That's not a bad idea."

"Shh. Better not tell me. I'm the enemy," she couldn't help saying.

Brock gave a heavy sigh. "You're not the enemy."

"Bet you'd never let me in the office again," she said.

"Sure I would," he said. "Just not right away. Dinner at home?" he asked, clearly changing the subject.

"If we must," she said.

"You hate it there," he concluded.

"It's so—" she searched for the right word "—full."

"I know," he said. "Maybe we could get rid of some of the clutter."

"How do you think your mother would feel about that?"

"It's possible she wouldn't even notice."

Elle snorted, then tried to cough to cover it. "I don't think so."

"Well, start with one room downstairs. Take it over and redo it the way you want. Put the old stuff in storage."

Elle felt a trickle of excitement. "This might work."

"Of course it will work," he said. "It was my suggestion."

She rolled her eyes. "You're so arrogant."

"That never stopped you before," he said.

She sucked in a quick breath. "No," she whispered. "It didn't."

"What do your want for dinner tonight?"

What she wanted more than anything was a quiet dinner in Brock's apartment at the office. But she knew that wasn't possible. He wouldn't let her near the office yet. She felt a deep sense of loss. They'd shared so many private memories there. "I'd like some good old American cooking tonight," she said, thinking of one of the few places they'd actually gone to together—a diner with a delicious defiance against the carb-hating trend of the day.

"Mashed potatoes," he said, and she heard the smile in his voice. "The Four Square Diner. Don't spend too much time at the outlets. I'll call later to firm up a time," he said and hung up.

Elle glanced at the sexy leopard-printed sheath hanging

on the end of the rack. She wondered if she would ever be able to inspire Brock's primal urges again.

After a jam-packed day, Brock stood to greet Elle at The Four Square Diner. He studied her face. "You overdid it today," he said. "You're tired."

She brushed her lips against his cheek. "Thank you. You look gorgeous, too," she said and sat down.

He couldn't keep his lips from twitching. "You're supposed to stay rested."

She picked up the menu from the table. "There's a difference between rested and going into a coma. How was your afternoon?"

"Good. The campaign for the Prentice account is going smoothly," he said.

"Great. How do you like your new assistant?"

"He isn't you," Brock said.

She nearly dropped her menu. "You have a male assistant?" she asked, surprised.

"Careful," Brock said. "You're edging toward sexist."

"The whole advertising business is sexist," she said dismissively. "I wasn't aware you'd ever had a male assistant."

"I haven't," Brock said. "But this one is competent."

"It might also negate any criticisms about your marriage to me," she said. "Good strategy."

Brock met her gaze, giving nothing away. The waitress arrived and took their order. After she left, Brock returned his attention to Elle. "What did you buy today?"

"Odds and ends," she said, wondering how much

of an embarrassment he considered her to be. She'd often thought her grandfather had considered her an embarrassment until he'd found a use for her.

"What odds? What ends?" he asked. "Just tell me you bought a new robe that you won't trip over."

She smiled. "Yes, I did, along with a few other things. Do you have plans for this weekend?"

Brock shrugged. "The usual," he said. "Work."

She nodded. "There's always that."

She noticed him lift his hand to a man across the room. She recognized the man as one of Brock's executives, Logan Emerson. The man nodded at Brock, glanced at her, then looked away. She'd always had an odd feeling about Logan. Brock hadn't discussed his hiring with her and she'd always wondered at Brock's motivation for bringing him into such a high-profile position at Maddox. Logan had never seemed to fit in.

"How's he doing with the other account reps now?" she asked.

"Fine," Brock said. "I've altered his duties a bit in the last few days. I think that will work out better."

"Oh, really?" she asked. "What will he be doing?"

"I've assigned him to work more closely with personnel and computer security," he said as their meal arrived.

"Wow," she said. "That's a big switch from sales."

He nodded but didn't make any further comment and a possibility occurred to her. "Computer security," she mused. "He always seemed better suited for security. So quiet, so determined to stay in the background—he could be a private investigator."

Brock's jaw twitched, but he still added nothing. It suddenly hit her.

"He *is* a private investigator," she said. "Was he the one who told you about me?"

Brock stabbed his fork into his meatloaf. "And if he was?" he asked her.

She bit her lip, feeling her appetite for the open-faced turkey sandwich disappear. She adjusted her paper napkin. "That's why you wouldn't talk about him with me," she said. "Did you already suspect me?"

Brock set down his fork. "You were the last person I suspected," he said, his eyes as turbulent as a stormy sea.

She felt a twist of guilt and looked away. "I was almost relieved when you found out," she confessed in a low voice. "Being pregnant made it even worse. If it hadn't been for my mother needing the experimental treatments—"

"What?" he asked, his voice hoarse. "What experimental treatments?"

She finally met his gaze. "I wasn't sure if Logan might have known something about my mother's illness," she said. "My mother is taking experimental treatments that are very expensive. There's no way she or I could afford them, and insurance wouldn't cover them."

"Are you saying that Athos agreed to pay for your mother's treatments as long as you spied on me?"

A lump formed in her throat. "Yes, he did. I'm ashamed of it, but I didn't feel as if I had any other choice. I couldn't risk losing her. She's all I've ever had."

The sound of stainless steel clanging against plates

and the conversation of the other diners was a roar compared to the absolute silence between them.

"Why didn't you tell me your mother was sick?" he asked.

She shook her head. "I didn't want to." She closed her eyes, thinking back to the times she'd shared with Brock. "I didn't want my time with you tainted with any of my problems. Those moments we shared together—it was like you and I were on a private island and nothing or no one could trespass." She opened her eyes and took a deep breath. "Afterward, I had my work and you had yours, but that time together was precious. It had to be protected."

Brock reached across the table, his hand covering hers. "I can take care of your mother's medical treatments."

She immediately shook her head, swallowing a quick taste of bitterness at the havoc her grandfather had created in her life. "No," she said. "Let him pay. It's the least he can do for all the trouble he has caused."

Brock's gaze gentled. "You're lucky you have such a good relationship with your mother," he said. "I admire your devotion to her."

Five

After a long shower, Elle wrapped a towel around herself and ran the blow dryer through her hair. She would clip the tags off her new robe in just a moment, she promised herself, looking forward to the luxurious sensation of silk over her skin. She suspected there'd be no sensual pleasures in her near future. They were, after all, sleeping in separate rooms.

Closing her eyes and mind to her thoughts, she concentrated on the warm air dancing through her hair and over her shoulders. A few seconds passed and she opened her eyes, finding Brock standing in front of her, bare-chested with a small tray in one of his hands.

Startled, she dropped the dryer. "Oh, my," she said, bending down to turn it off. As she leaned forward, her towel dropped to her waist. Swearing under her breath, she lifted it to cover her chest and stood.

"I knocked," he said, his gaze sliding across her towel-covered body.

"I didn't hear you," she said, sensing awareness twist and turn between them. She felt heat rush to her face.

"I was downstairs and the housekeeper thought you might like some juice and cookies," he said.

Elle smiled and took the small tray from him. Still holding on to her towel, she carefully set it on the dresser. "That was nice. She's so sweet, but she fusses over me more than my mother."

"Maybe because you're so busy taking care of your mother," he said.

"Maybe," she said, too aware of his presence so close to her. She knew his body intimately. At the moment, he wore a pair of pajama bottoms that dipped below his ripped abs and belly button. She remembered sliding her hands over his wide shoulders while he kissed her deeply. It was all too easy to recall the sexy gasp he made when she touched him intimately.

"Elle," Brock said. "What are you thinking right now?"

She bit her lip and looked away. "Nothing important. Nothing worth—"

He touched her arm and her denial stuck in her throat. It had been two weeks since they'd been intimate, and God help her, she'd missed him. Even through the morning sickness. She'd missed being with him, away from everything and everyone else.

"I can't believe you still want me," she whispered.

He pulled her toward him and the sensation of his strong chest against her nearly buckled her knees. She deliberately stiffened them.

"Why not?" he asked. He skimmed his hand down to the small of her back and pressed her into him.

The obvious strength of his arousal shocked her. She searched his gaze for clues to his emotions. "But after what I did," she said. "How could—"

He moved his other hand up to the back of her head, sliding his fingers through her hair, tilting her head so that her mouth was completely accessible to him. "Let's not overthink it."

He lowered his mouth to hers and kissed her possessively. Should she be asking for more than sex? she wondered. Maybe not, she thought as his tongue slid past her lips and caressed hers. Maybe he was right. Maybe she should stop thinking and concentrate on feeling. What did she have to lose?

Dropping the towel, she lifted her hands to the back of his neck and surrendered to the moment.

Brock gave a low, barely audible growl and pushed the towel to the floor. When her bare breasts pressed against his chest, she sighed. He groaned. He slid one of his hands over her nipple and she gasped, feeling a correlating electricity between her legs.

"Problem?" he asked, rubbing his lips over hers.

"I'm more sensitive since I'm—" He rubbed her nipple again and she sucked in another breath as she felt herself grow swollen.

"Should I stop?"

"Oh, please, no," she said, surprised at the speed of her arousal.

"Is this safe for you?" he asked, going completely still. "For the baby?"

She nodded. "The doctor said—" She licked her lips. "He said we can do anything we did before."

Brock swore under his breath and lifted his hands to her face. "Damn my soul, but I've missed you," he said and took her mouth in a sensual, ferocious kiss that matched the way she felt about him.

With each second that passed, she felt her temperature rise, her heart beat faster. She wanted more, so much more. Squeezing the muscles of his arms and drawing his tongue into her mouth, she couldn't keep still. She wriggled against him and he slid his leg between hers, lifting it high between her thighs, rubbing her where she was already wet and aching.

She slid her hands down over his ribs to his flat abdomen and pushed her fingers beneath the waistband of his drawstring pants. Brock lifted his hand to her breasts, flicking his thumbs over her nipples.

The sensation made her dizzy. She pushed his pants over his hips, wanting more of him, craving ultimate closeness.

"It's too fast," he muttered as she closed her hand over his shaft.

"Not for me," she said.

"Oh, Elle," he said, picking her up in his arms and carrying her into his bedroom. He set her on his big bed and pushed his pants the rest of the way down. His gaze fixed on hers.

"You don't know how many times I've dreamed about having you in my bed here," he muttered and slid his hand between her thighs, finding her secret wetness. His mouth dipped to hers, his tongue taunting and exploring the same way his fingers were teasing her femininity, making her breathless and almost shockingly needy for him.

The wanting in her tightened like a strong coil, pushing her higher and higher. She stroked desperately at his flexed arms and shoulders. His harsh breaths mingled with hers.

"Brock," she said, a mixture of a plea and demand.

One second later, he slid inside. His gaze, dark with arousal, held hers as he thrust. Unable to hold back, she arched toward him and felt herself come apart in fits and starts. He kept thrusting, driving her higher than she'd thought possible until one last time, he stiffened inside her and his climax vibrated all the way to her core.

She held on tight, stunned by the ferocity of their lovemaking. His heart pounded against hers and his breath blew over her bare shoulder. She felt his strength and power in every cell of her being and never wanted to let go of the sensation.

After a few more breaths, he let out a long sigh and eased to his side, still holding her in his arms. "From now on," he said, "you'll sleep in here with me."

The next morning, Elle was awakened by a sound. She opened her eyes to the sight of Brock dressed and picking up his BlackBerry from its charger. A tiny ray of sunlight peeked through the shade on the window.

Shaking off her sleepiness, she sat up. "Where are you going?"

He glanced at her. "Where I go almost every Saturday," he said. "To the office. I need to review some new suggestions that came in yesterday for one of our major accounts. No need for you to get up. I'll be back late this afternoon. Enjoy your day," he said and walked out of the room.

Elle stared after him, stunned at his perfunctory attitude. Frowning, she halfway wondered if he was the same man who'd made love to her with such passion last night. Last night he'd acted as if he couldn't get enough of her. Today he acted as if he couldn't get away from her fast enough.

She'd felt the enormous connection between them click back into place last night. She'd been sure their lovemaking represented a turning point. Now she wasn't sure at all. Brock was so distant. Even when they'd been having their affair in the office, he'd acted warmer than this. She instinctively wrapped her arms around herself as if she felt a sudden chill.

He still didn't trust her, she realized, feeling a knot form in her stomach. She shouldn't be surprised. Even though he had sold her on the idea that they could overcome what she had done for the sake of the baby, he clearly wasn't there yet. She couldn't help wondering if he ever would be. Sinking back down onto the bed, she dozed for a while, trying to escape her lost, afraid feelings. After some bizarre dreams, Elle threw off the covers and jumped out of bed. She refused to be a wuss. There were much worse things she could be facing. Now wasn't the time to cower under the covers. Now was time to try to make her marriage work, and she'd start with the house. Today she would work on redoing the den.

The first thing she ditched was the heavy drapes. The housekeeper gasped when she saw Elle on a chair, pulling them down.

"Mrs. Maddox, what on earth are you doing?" Anna asked.

"Brock told me to pick a room and redecorate it. I've chosen this one," she said.

The housekeeper's eyes widened. "Oh, my. Has he, uh, discussed this with the senior Mrs. Maddox?"

"I don't think so," Elle said. "But he said he didn't think his mother would mind if I redid one room. It won't be as if I'm taking over the entire house."

"True," the housekeeper said, nodding. The rest of her expression didn't agree with her nod.

Elle sighed. "Do you think I shouldn't? I don't want to offend her."

"Technically, the house belongs to Mr. Maddox. Mrs. Maddox has lived here since her husband passed away, but by all rights, Mr. Maddox is the master of the house and since you're his wife, your wishes should be respected."

"A roundabout way of saying there could be trouble," Elle said, then lifted her hand. "Don't worry. I don't expect you to comment. No need for divided loyalty." She turned her attention back to the room. "I'll try to tie in some of the colors from the other rooms, but I want to make this room comfortable for Brock. I want him to feel like he can relax here."

"I think that's an excellent idea," Anna said.

"The drapes have got to go, though," Elle said. "And most of the furniture and knickknacks."

"As you wish," the housekeeper said. "But please let Roger do it. Mr. Maddox would have my head if he saw you on that chair."

Elle spent the next several hours packing up knickknacks while Roger hauled away anything that weighed more than a tissue.

"I don't want to impose, but if you would like some suggestions, Mrs. Maddox used some decorators," the housekeeper said.

"Thank you. I could use some suggestions, but I know someone who has a great eye and I owe her a visit," she said, thinking of Bree Kincannon Spencer. Bree's friendship was another casualty in the dirty little corporate war her grandfather had instigated. Although Elle knew Bree might not forgive her, she needed to apologize to the woman who had trusted and befriended her. The prospect made her nervous, but it was necessary. "This is a lot of furniture. Are you sure you can find a place to store it?"

Roger nodded. "No problem. We'll find a place."

"Thank you," Elle said and smiled. "Both of you." Then she went upstairs to her room and dialed Bree's cell, expecting to leave a message that might very well be ignored.

"Hello?" Bree said breathlessly after several rings.

Surprised at the sound of the woman's voice, Elle temporarily lost her words.

"Hello?" Bree repeated. "Elle?"

"Yes, it's me," Elle said, pacing from one end of the bedroom to the other. "Listen, I know you probably hate me. If I were you, I would hate me, too, but would you be willing to give me a few minutes of your time to explain? Nothing will excuse what I did, but your friendship really meant a lot to me. I would just like you to know what really happened."

Silence stretched from the other side of the line,

making Elle's stomach knot. "I understand if you don't want to, and I know you're probably busy with Gavin today, since it's a Saturday—"

"I sent Gavin to play golf," Bree said. "He needed to take a break from his new business and I know he's missed playing but he didn't want me to feel neglected. I had to insist."

"You're so lucky," Elle said in a low voice, thinking of how Brock had left before she'd even made it out of bed that morning.

"I could probably meet you in an hour. Gavin won't be back until five. There's a little café down the street from us. Would you like to meet there?"

"Yes, thank you, Bree. This means a lot to me," Elle said.

An hour later, Elle walked into the café, spotting Bree at a table. The young woman stood and Elle immediately saw a new confidence in her. Elle remembered when Bree had enlisted her help with a makeover to get Gavin's attention. Bree had spent so many years without self-confidence that she hadn't realized what a true beauty she was. But now she was a radiant, happily married woman—and a woman who had been betrayed by Elle. Elle felt another twist of nerves ripple through her.

"Bree, thank you for coming." Elle's voice trembled, but she was determined. "I'm so, so terribly sorry for what I've done," she said, and then the whole story about her grandfather and her mother's illness just spilled out.

Fifteen minutes later, Bree reached for Elle's hand. "Oh, my God. How terrible. Why didn't you tell me?"

she asked. "I would have helped. You know I have the money."

"I couldn't," Elle said. "And I felt so trapped and afraid. Every day looking in the mirror, I just hated myself more and more. And then when Brock and I got involved—" Elle felt her voice break again.

Bree looked at her in sympathy. "Gavin told me Brock looked devastated when he got the news from the P.I."

Even though deep down, Elle had suspected that Brock would have been hurt by the news, part of her had wondered if it might have stabbed his ego more than his heart. Now, she couldn't be sure.

"Well, the good news is that you and Brock are married, so everything is fixed," Bree said cheerfully.

Elle didn't say anything, but Bree must have read her expression.

"What's wrong? Brock must have forgiven you, right?"

"It's not that easy," Elle said. "We're working on things." She bit her lip. "I'm pregnant," she whispered.

Bree's eyes rounded. "Oh, my goodness. Are you excited? Is he? I mean, I know it's been a muddy swim getting here, but a *baby*."

Elle realized more than ever how much she had missed Bree during the last few weeks. "I'm getting there," she said. "I'm just getting over morning sickness."

"As someone whose marriage didn't start out perfectly, the only thing I can say is hold on. Things can change for the better. They certainly did for me. For a while there, I never believed Gavin would love me, but I wouldn't doubt it for a second now."

"I'm so glad. You really do deserve happiness," Elle said.

Bree shot her a sympathetic smile. "You do, too, Elle."

"Do you think you can ever forgive me?" Elle asked.

"It's already done. But you're going to need to forgive yourself, too."

Elle felt a slight easing in her chest. She'd carried around the tight feeling so long it had become a part of her. To have Bree forgive her so freely gave her hope that maybe she and Brock could make their family work after all.

"Thank you so much, Bree," she said. "And now I have a favor to ask. You remember how I helped you with your little makeover?"

Bree nodded. "You definitely don't need a makeover."

"Brock's den needs a makeover. You have a wonderful eye. I was hoping you wouldn't mind helping me."

"I'm flattered," Bree said. "Of course I'll help."

After taking photographs of the den and talking about ideas, Elle and Bree decided to go shopping and found the perfect couch, a recliner for Brock and a sofa table. Unaccustomed to having things delivered at the drop of a dime, Elle blinked at how Bree arranged to get the furniture delivered immediately. Bree left with a hug and Elle went to an electronics store to purchase a huge television. As soon as she mentioned her address, the store manager agreed to deliver and set it up immediately.

By seven thirty, she was propped on the new sofa, watching a chick flick on the new television while she ate roasted chicken, green beans and macaroni and cheese. The sad thing was that Brock still hadn't come home. Elle consoled herself with the macaroni and cheese, even though she knew she would rue the effect later.

Just before eight o'clock, Brock strode into the room, glancing around in surprise. "Where'd the furniture go?"

"You told me to redo a room," she said. "This is the room I've chosen."

He glanced at the television. "That's a great picture. I bet you would feel like you're at the game when you're watching baseball," he said.

"That's the idea," she said, pleased with her purchase. "Do you mind trying out your new chair?" she asked, waving her hand toward the recliner.

He gave a short laugh and moved to the chair, sitting down and easing back. He let out a sigh. "Perfect," he said.

Elle beamed. "I think I sat in fifty chairs before I chose that one."

"I like the couch, too," he said. "The room looks totally different."

"I'm not done with it yet, but I think I've made a good start."

He shot her an inquisitive glance. "You've been a busy girl."

She nodded. "Yes, I have."

He glanced at her plate. "And you're eating well, too. I'm glad to see it."

Elle sighed, looking at her mostly empty plate. "I'm craving carbs. Heaven help me when it's all over."

"You'll be a beautiful mother," he said quietly.

"Do you really think so?" she asked.

"Yes, I do," he said.

She wanted to ask him if he'd missed her today, if he'd thought of her at all, but she knew the question would sound silly. "How was your day?" she asked.

"Good. Fuller than I expected. I had dinner with a prospective client. The owner of a cosmetics company based on the west coast." He rose from the chair.

"Sounds exciting," she said, hoping he would tell her more.

"It's the beginning stages, so anything can happen. You know how it goes." His gaze fell over her like a warm veil of heat. "Come upstairs and we can relax in the hot tub."

The desire in his eyes temporarily dissolved her questions. She gave a slow shake of her head. "Pregnancy and hot tubs aren't a good idea. Something about the high temperatures being dangerous for the baby."

He nodded. "I see."

"But a bath or a shower is okay," she said.

He extended his hand. "Come upstairs with me," he said. "I've missed you."

Those last three words were pure magic to her.

On Sunday, Brock didn't go into the office and Elle persuaded him to go for a walk on the beach and share a picnic.

Brock leaned back against the quilt they'd spread

out on the sand. "I can't remember the last time I did this."

"Maybe you should do it more often," she said, packing away the remnants of their picnic lunch.

"Maybe," he said, his gaze skimming over her, taking a long swallow from his water bottle. "How are you adjusting to being a Maddox bride?"

"I'm getting there," she said. "I'm just hoping my husband will be home more when our child is born."

He inhaled and nodded thoughtfully. "I'm working on it. My father spent a lot more time at the office than he ever did with us."

"What do *you* want?" she asked. "More time in the office? Or more time with your child?"

"I hadn't even considered it until now," he said. "I was always too busy protecting and growing the company."

"I don't really know what to expect of a father," she said and shrugged, "because my father left as soon as he found out my mother was pregnant."

"That must have been tough for both of you," Brock said.

She nodded. "It was, but my mother and I were always very close, so I'm lucky that way. Unconditional love between us."

"But something tells me you had to take care of her a lot," Brock said.

"True," she admitted. "But with her, I always felt good enough. Did you ever feel that way with your father?"

"Hmm," he said. "Good question. I was always pushed to do better, do more." He glanced at her. "In that way, you were lucky." He rose up and leaned toward her, pressing his mouth against hers. "What inspired you to be such a hard worker?"

"I didn't want to be at the mercy of any man," she said. The answer came easily to her lips.

He lifted his eyebrows. "Really?"

"Yes. I spent my entire life with my grandfather supporting us though he was ashamed of us. I didn't want that for my future. I studied and worked hard," she said, then closed her eyes. "Then my mother got sick."

She felt him stroke her hand. "When did Koteas approach you?"

Bitterness filled her mouth. "When my mother's improvement dipped and the only thing that could help her was the experimental treatment. Of course, insurance wouldn't cover it. And my grandfather wouldn't cover it without a price."

"Did you plan to seduce me?"

Elle laughed and opened her eyes to meet his gaze. "That's one of the funniest things you've ever said to me. I was terrified you wouldn't hire me. When you finally did, I was fascinated by you. You were this unstoppable force. I'd never met anyone like you."

"You went to bed with me without a blink of an eye," he said.

"I—" She broke off, feeing a stab of guilt mixed with a myriad of other emotions. "I couldn't miss out on being with you," she said. "Why did you decide to be with me?"

"Same reason, different words," Brock said, sliding his hand behind her neck and drawing her mouth against his. "I couldn't resist you."

Six

"Oh, my God! Vandals have struck," a woman's shrill voice called.

Just out of the shower, Elle quickly wrapped her robe around her. Alarmed, she pushed open her door and raced—carefully—down the stairs.

Another shriek sounded from the area of the den.

Elle finally made it there in bare feet and gaped at Brock's enraged mother, Carol. "Oh, my God," the sophisticated, elegant woman repeated.

"It wasn't a vandal," Elle said breathlessly. "It was me."

Carol looked at her and frowned as much as her Botox-treated brow would allow. "Who are you?"

Elle fought a flutter of nerves. "I'm Elle," she said. "Elle Linton—"

"Linton," Carol interjected. "That name is familiar.

Don't tell me," she said, lifting her hand when Elle opened her mouth to speak. "I know that name." She blinked in recognition. "My son Brock's assistant." Then she frowned again. "Why are you here? And wearing a robe? And destroying my den?" Carol said, looking around the room in complete disapproval.

Elle paused, then said, "Elle Linton Maddox."

Carol's eyebrows would have risen to her hairline if they could have. "Maddox? Oh, my God. Has my son married you?" Her gaze immediately dipped to Elle's belly. "Are you pregnant?"

Elle cleared her throat, realizing that Brock hadn't bothered to contact his mother about their marriage. "Brock and I were married just last week."

"Oh," Carol said, clearly at a loss for words. "He didn't tell me."

Although Elle understood why Brock resisted his mother's involvement in both business and his personal life, she felt a twinge of sympathy for the woman. It couldn't be easy hearing that your oldest son had gotten married—from the new wife herself. "I'm sorry. I realize this is awkward," Elle said. "Brock has told me a lot about you."

Carol's lips lifted in a cynical smile. "All good, I'm sure," she said, looking at the den again. "I don't suppose you could tell me what has happened to this room."

"Uh, Brock asked me to choose one room downstairs to redecorate." Elle shrugged. "I chose the den."

"Oh," Carol said. "I suppose I shouldn't be surprised. It was bound to happen someday." She returned her attention to Elle, studying her for a long moment. "So you're the new Maddox bride," Carol said, slowly strolling toward her. "I suspect you have no idea what you're getting into, but I can help with that. My flight from Aspen just arrived an hour ago—I made an extra stop there on my way back from Europe. Let me freshen up and the two of us can do lunch."

Uncomfortable at the prospect, Elle shook her head. "Oh, I couldn't. You just got in. I'm sure you want to relax."

"Nonsense," Carol said, lifting her lips in a smile that didn't meet her eyes. "I need to get to know my son's new wife." She glanced down at Elle's abdomen again. "You didn't answer my question. Are you pregnant?"

Elle thought about denying it because she knew what Carol would think—that the pregnancy was the only reason Brock had married her. Which, of course, was true. "Yes, I am."

Carol gave a knowing nod. She glanced down at a diamond-encrusted watch. "Will an hour give you enough time to get ready?"

"That's plenty of time, thank you," Elle said. "But if you need to do something else, there's no rush—"

Carol smiled again. "There's nothing more important."

An hour later, Elle joined Carol in the Bentley driven by a driver named Dirk. Carol peppered her with questions during the ride, and Elle did her best to sound as boring as possible. The car pulled in front of a posh restaurant in a pricey shopping neighborhood.

"Here we are," Carol said and led the way into the restaurant. Although there was a lunchtime crowd, the host wasted no time finding a table for them. "Now," she said. "Tell me all about yourself. All about your romance with my son."

Grateful for the water the server immediately poured, Elle shrugged. "It wasn't something either of us expected. There was just this special connection we couldn't ignore."

"Obviously, since you're already pregnant. How far along are you?"

"Over three months," Elle said, trying to ignore Carol's tone. "But I'd rather hear more about you and the family. What was Brock like as a baby?" Elle said. "I'm sure you must have so many stories to share."

"Not as many as you'd think. Being the wife of James Maddox was a full-time job. My husband expected me to be by his side for client dinners. I joined clubs and served on boards to keep the Maddox name visible. The company was always number one with my husband. As it will be with Brock," she said. "But I'm sure you already know that, since you've worked with him."

"But you must have some memories of Brock as a child," Elle said.

"He was a handful. Very physically active, very curious, ambitious from the day he was born. Of course, his father loved that about him. We had a nanny before he was sent to private school. His father had very strong opinions about Brock's upbringing. He always said he was raising the lead lion, and the word 'average' was never allowed in any discussions about Brock. Speaking of a nanny, I can get you in with the most exclusive agency in San Francisco."

"Oh, I haven't even thought about nannies yet," Elle

said, thinking her view of parenting might differ widely from that of Carol Maddox.

"Well, don't leave it until it's too late. I'm sure Brock will demand the cream of the crop. He's just like his father that way," Carol said. "Since you're no longer working for Brock, have you decided which clubs you'd like to join? I can help you with that, too."

Elle shrugged and smiled, trying not to feel overwhelmed. "I have to be honest. Between the marriage, the move and the pregnancy, I'm still taking it one day at a time."

"Oh, the pregnancy," Carol said and shook her head. "The most miserable times of my life. I was in bed half the time with both of them. Maybe you'll get lucky and have a boy the first time and then you can talk Brock into stopping at one. Having a second child was necessary for the well-being of my marriage," Carol added. "Never forget for a moment that women will compete for the attention of a wealthy man, whether he's married or not. There's always someone trying to take your husband away from you."

When Elle returned home, she felt like crawling back into bed and hiding. Marrying Brock was clearly the biggest mistake of her life. She should have quit Maddox and fled to Mexico or Canada or Paris. Anywhere but here with Brock's Cruella de Vil mother. Feeling suffocated, Elle snuck out of the house and drove to her mother's. They spent the afternoon talking and baking cookies together for one of the members of Suzanne's support group.

When the clock passed seven in the evening, her

mother slid her arm around Elle. "Sweetie, shouldn't you be with your husband?"

"He's working. He won't mind me spending time with you," Elle said.

"But it's getting late," her mother said. "Are you sure you shouldn't go home?"

Elle's cell phone rang. She winced, pretty certain she knew who was calling.

"Elle?" her mother prompted, when she didn't race to her purse.

Elle reached for her phone and answered it. "Hi," she said.

"Where are you?" Brock asked.

"With my mom," Elle said, forcing her lips into a smile. "Baking cookies. Where are you?"

"At home looking for my wife," Brock said. He paused a half beat. "My mother scared the piss out of you, didn't she?"

Elle laughed nervously. "Cannot lie. She's a little creepy."

"Come home," he said. "I'll protect you."

"You can't protect me during the day when you're at work," she said.

"I can buy her a new place," he said. "Let her fill it up with all the stuff that's in the house."

"She can't be all bad," Elle said. "She had you."

"Don't remind me," he muttered.

"I don't know," Elle said. "I bet you don't know everything about what went on between her and your father."

"You're not defending her," he said.

"No, but I think there may be more than meets the eye."

"I can't disagree. There's Botox, face-lifts, Restylane—"

"Give the woman a break. Her whole life was being Mrs. James Maddox."

"She sucked you in," Brock said.

"I can see some of her points," she admitted.

Silence passed. "You're joking."

"No. I'm not."

"That's it," Brock said. "I'm sending Roger to get you."

"I have my car," Elle said.

"I don't want you driving in the dark," Brock said.

Elle rolled her eyes. "Too bad," she said and hung up. Feeling her mother's gaze on her, she pretended to continue her conversation. "Of course, I'll come home darling. Right away," she said and turned to her mother. "I guess I should go home."

Her mother studied her suspiciously. "Are you sure everything is okay between the two of you?"

"I'm sure," Elle fibbed, making sure not to look directly at her mother because her mother could read her like a book. "We're newlyweds. We're working things out. Plus, I'm pregnant. It's complicated, but Brock is an amazing man." Elle wasn't shading the truth about most of what she'd said. "I'll see you soon," she said and gave her mother a hug.

Thirty minutes later, Brock heard the front door open. He knew it was Elle and breathed a sigh of relief. If he'd known his mother was returning today, he would have found a way to protect Elle. His mother was the most manipulative woman he'd ever met and he would have thrown her out of the house earlier except he'd never had a compelling reason. Until now.

He strode toward the foyer and met Elle just as she took her first step upstairs. "Elle," he said.

She turned around. "Hi," she said.

"I'm sorry you had to deal with my mother by yourself today," he said.

She made a face. "It's not as if she's a mass murderer," Elle said. "Although she clearly has issues."

"That's an understatement," he muttered. "I'll be moving her out as soon as possible."

Elle frowned.

"What?" he demanded.

"I hate to displace her," Elle said. "Something about her seems so sad."

Seeing the compassion on her face made something inside him twist and turn. Underneath it all, Elle had a good heart, but her sympathy for Carol was misplaced. "Giving Carol her own place isn't displacing her. It's not as if I'm kicking her out and telling her to live in a park."

Elle bit her lip. "Are you sure it's the most compassionate thing to do?"

"I'm sure it's the right thing to do, for Carol and our marriage," he said firmly.

Two days later, Carol was ensconced in a new home just a few streets over and all her things had been hauled away by a moving company. Unfortunately, she had taken very few of the furnishings from Brock's home, which meant that Elle would need to sort out what should be discarded and what should be kept.

Elle turned to Anna. "What if I throw away something important, something that belonged to James?"

Anna pressed her lips together in sympathy. "I'll help as best I can, but he did pass several years ago."

Elle groaned. "I'll run everything past you. If there are questions about something, we'll put it in storage."

Going through all the junk took over twelve hours a day for the next week. Elle fell into bed every night exhausted. When Brock awakened her one morning, she wasn't sure which day of the week it was.

"This has got to stop," he said. "It's bad for your health. Bad for the baby."

"It's almost done. It'll probably only take a couple more days" she said, still melting into the mattress.

She felt his sigh drift over her shoulders. "I still have a lot to do with Prentice, and we're on the brink of another big deal, but I'd like to take you away," he said, skimming his fingers through her hair.

"Really?" she said. "Where?"

"Somewhere quiet," he said. "Somewhere away from here."

"I tried to exorcise the demons in this house, but I'm not sure I did," Elle said.

"Demons?" Brock echoed.

"Bad karma?" she said. "Bad memories? I'm not sure what it is, but I don't want it contaminating our future," she murmured.

He took her shoulders and turned her over to face him. He looked into her sleepy blue eyes and found himself craving more. "There's no such thing as bad karma," he told her. "I told you I would protect you."

She let out a long sigh. "With our histories, it's going to take more than one warrior to make our marriage work."

He saw the steely determination in her gaze and felt a surge of something primitive inside him. He'd never met a woman like Elle, a woman who could match his passion and his strength. "You keep surprising me."

"Is that a good thing?" she asked, her blue eyes dark and moody.

"I'll let you know. In the meantime, pack a bag. You and I are getting out of here," he said, making an instant decision. If Elle was going to rest, then he needed to take her away.

Within hours, Brock was driving toward the mountains. "I have a house a few hours from town. I go there as often as I can, which hasn't been much lately."

She sank into her leather seat and relaxed. "I've never heard about this place. You never went when I worked for you."

"When you were working for me, I was spending every spare moment I could with you," he said, taking a turn up a mountain road.

She rolled her head toward him. "It's nice to know that I wasn't the only one who was half crazed," she said.

He shot her a glance, then chuckled under his breath. "Half crazed is under estimating it by a long shot."

"Yeah, yeah," she said. "At least you got to stay all night in your apartment. I usually had to drive home in the middle of the night."

"What are you talking about? My driver took you home," he said.

"Oops," she said.

He shot her a sideways glance, feeling his gut tighten with frustration. "Are you telling me Dirk didn't take you home all those times?"

She paused. "I'm not telling you that."

"Because you don't want him fired," Brock said. "How the hell did you talk him out of it?"

"It wasn't easy, but how was I going to explain arriving home at my mother's with a chauffeur, especially when I needed to drive myself to the office the next day? He followed me to make sure I arrived home safely."

"I guess I shouldn't be surprised. Dirk did the right thing by following you home," Brock said. "I never realized what a stubborn streak you have."

"When I worked for you, my job was to make sure I anticipated your every need to make your life as easy as possible," she said. "Now I'm your wife."

"You mean the job description has changed," he said, and chuckled.

Silence stretched between them and he shot a quick glance at her. She looked pensive. "Elle, what's wrong?"

"I worry about how we're going to negotiate everything. I'm not like your mother," she said.

"Thank God," he said.

"What I mean is, I'm not the corporate super-wife type. If you married me expecting me to agree with your every thought, then we're going to have some problems. Do you realize that you and I haven't even discussed parenting? Based on what your mother said, your father was determined to raise you as some kind of super Maddox CEO. I can tell you now that I want our child to have a much more balanced upbringing."

Offended by her assessment of his father, Brock tightened his hands on the steering wheel. "My father made sure I had the best of everything, the best education—"

"The best nanny," Elle interjected. "What if I don't want a nanny raising my child? What if I don't want my child sent away to boarding school?"

Hearing fear and panic in Elle's voice, Brock realized where all this was coming from and took a mind-calming breath. "Carol's got you all worked up for nothing. You should know that she loves causing trouble. I think she was just trying to intimidate you, Elle."

"She brought up some important issues, Brock. For one thing, I'm not going to sign on to a bunch of high-brow clubs and societies if it means our child will be getting leftovers from me. Tell the truth. When you married me, didn't you expect me to step into a role just like your mother did?"

Brock shook his head, feeling something inside him twist and tighten, angry that his mother had made an already challenging situation more difficult. "I honestly didn't think that far," he said. "I just knew that I wanted us to do the right thing for the baby, and that meant getting married."

Elle was silent again for a long moment. "Well, you can check that off your list," she said. "But there are other things we'll need to settle."

He raked his hand through his hair in frustration. "She's always causing trouble," he muttered. "Thank

God she's out of the house now. You'll see soon enough that everything will work out." Brock would make sure of it. He may have had one failed engagement, but there would be no failed marriage. "Relax. It's time for you to take a break."

Despite the worries sprouting like weeds in her mind, Elle dozed off. As they pulled into a clearing, she got her first glimpse of the mountain chalet, and the serene setting immediately eased some of her tensions. "It's beautiful," she said. "So peaceful."

"It was a mess when I first bought it. I redid the whole thing." He nodded toward the chalet. "A caretaker looks after it while I'm gone and stocks the refrigerator when I tell him I'm on my way. His wife usually prepares a couple of meals for me and leaves them in the freezer for reheating, so we won't have to cook."

"You've seemed so restless and busy since I've met you. It's hard for me to imagine you being able to relax enough to enjoy this. What's the longest amount of time you've ever stayed here?" she asked as he pulled to a stop.

"A week in the winter. There's a ski resort not far. I spent another week working on it during one summer. And then I came up here every weekend for a while," he said. "But I bought it more for short breaks. Come on. I want to show you inside."

He got out of the car and led her to the front porch, where a wooden swing hung from the roof. Two rocking chairs and a table echoed the cozy, laid-back ambience. She followed him through the front door to a foyer that was two stories high. Light spilled in through the tall windows onto the tile floors dotted with soft rugs. The natural flow of the house led her to a large room filled with brown leather couches and chairs, golden wood tables and an HDTV that bore a strong resemblance to the one she'd chosen for the den in Brock's home.

She met his gaze and laughed. "It's the same size as the one I got, isn't it?"

He smiled and took her hand. "You must know my taste," he said, lifting her hand to his mouth.

Her heart skittered at his charming maneuver. She knew he had plenty of charm, but he'd displayed little of it toward her during the last few weeks. Understandably so.

"Come outside," he said. "The view will take your breath away."

He led her out glass doors to a two-story deck that revealed peaks and valleys as far as the eye could see. "It's amazing. It's so wonderful, I'm surprised you're not up here nearly every weekend."

"There've been too many demands at work," he said, staring at the view. "Especially over the last several months."

Elle felt a stab and twist of guilt. "Because of me," she said.

His gaze flickered, but he didn't look at her. "It's water under the bridge," he said. "I have to focus on repairing damage and making sure the company is secure and ready for the future."

More than ever, she hated that she had made Brock's job even more demanding and difficult than it should have been. She put her hand on his arm. "I really am sorry," she said.

He shrugged away. "Like I said, we can't focus on that. We have to move on. Speaking of which, let me show you the rest of the house."

She slipped her hand inside his, wishing she could get beneath the surface of Brock's veneer. Although she'd suspected he'd let her closer than most, she still sensed that he kept a protective wall around his heart. For example, she knew nothing about his failed engagement. She hesitated to talk about it, but she was growing impatient with the secrets between them. Plunging into uncharted territory, she glanced up at him. "Did you ever bring your ex-fiancée here?" she asked softly.

He glanced at her in surprise and shook his head. "No. I thought about it, but there was never time. Claire didn't understand the demands of my position. She wanted a man who could take off and travel whenever she felt the urge. I couldn't be that man. It wasn't all her fault, though. Toward the end, I could tell things weren't going to work out between us and I buried myself in my job even more."

"Was the breakup difficult for you?"

He gave a wry smile. "I don't like to fail," he said. "At anything. I'd had a crush on her during college, but she was always in a relationship with someone else. We bumped into each other when she was finally single and I decided I'd finally gotten my chance."

Elle's heart twisted at the idea of Brock waiting so long for a woman. He hadn't had to wait any time at all for Elle. She'd tumbled head over heels for him right away. "If you had loved her so long, how could you let her go?"

"She wasn't happy. Besides, I'm not sure I would call

it love back in college. It was more a case of unrequited lust then. The dream and reality didn't match up. We weren't well suited."

Digesting his explanation, she smiled cautiously in return. "And you think you and I *are* well suited?" she asked.

"Things are only going to get better for you and me. Trust me," he said.

Walking into the large master bedroom with the same beautiful view as the deck downstairs, she watched him meet her gaze with pride. "Not bad, is it? I put money down on this place after I'd been working for my father for three years and had won a new account. He was pissed that I hadn't consulted him first."

"I don't think you needed to consult with anyone about this," she said. "It's your secret baby, isn't it?"

He lifted an eyebrow. "That's an interesting way of putting it," he said, glancing out the window.

"Well, it is. How many people have you told about this place?" she asked.

"Not many. My brother knows about it."

"Your one act of rebellion," she said.

"Oh, I rebelled more than once. This was just my most productive act of rebellion," he said.

"Did your father ever see it after you renovated it?"

His eyes narrowed. "No. My father was a great man, but he never liked to admit when he was wrong."

"You don't have that trait," she said. "That was one of the things that drew me to you. You are extremely confident, and can made decisions at the speed of lightning. So many of the decisions you made when we were working together, I would have second- or third-guessed.

But you went ahead and made them. In the rare moments when you were wrong, you admitted it and took another track."

"The ad business requires decisiveness. If you stay in the same place too long, you'll get run over. I have too many people counting on me to allow that to happen," he said, meeting her gaze with laser-blue intensity. "I can't let them down."

He would never allow himself to let them down, just as he would never surrender the responsibility of his child. His sense of obligation was fierce and steadfast. She felt a shudder ripple through her at his expression and she found herself wondering if he would be the compassionate father she hoped he would be, or the hard taskmaster his father had been for him.

"Are you hungry?" he asked. "I called ahead and the caretaker said he would put cold cuts in the refrigerator for us. After that, perhaps you'd like to rest again."

"A sandwich sounds good, but I'd rather go for a hike than take a nap. I can nap in San Francisco," she said.

"Not that I could see," he said. "According to Anna, you were barely taking breaks for meals during the last week."

"I'm surrounded by tattletales," she said in frustration. "You have these people watching me like hawks."

"I'm your husband now, Elle. It's my responsibility to make sure you're safe and well-cared for. "

Responsibility. Obligation. Duty. She didn't want to be any of those to Brock, but she was certain he wouldn't understand her gripe, especially since she was pregnant with his child.

"Sandwich and hike, then," she said, lifting her

chin. "You can take a nap if you're feeling tired," she suggested, unable to resist the urge to goad him a little.

He chuckled and pulled her toward him. "You've forgotten. You always fell asleep before I did at my apartment."

She lifted her hand in surrender. "I can't argue with that," she said as he planted a kiss on her mouth.

Several hours later, after lunch, hiking, and consuming a warmed-up chicken pot pie, Brock sat on the sofa and Elle brought him a scotch on the rocks. He noticed she did it as if she hadn't thought twice about it.

"Thanks," he said and studied her for a long moment. "It occurs to me that you may know more about my preferences than I know about yours," he said as she sank onto the couch beside him with a bottle of water.

"Hmm," she said and laughed with a self-satisfied smile. "You've never been anyone's assistant, let alone *my* assistant."

Brock took a sip of the perfectly chilled scotch. "You don't have to be arrogant about it," he said with a grin.

She slid a sideways glance at him. "I am not, nor have I ever been, arrogant. The concept is completely foreign to me."

"Okay, then you're a show-off," he said, taking another sip.

She dropped her jaw. "I am *not* a show-off. If anyone is a show-off, it's you," she said. "Look at you, with you laser-blue eyes and dark hair. You're charming when you're inclined…"

He frowned at her. "When I'm inclined?" he echoed.

"It's not every day," she said.

Brock shook his head. There were so many people who sucked up to him on a daily basis—but not Elle, and he liked her for that. "So what's your favorite cocktail?" he asked.

"Strawberry martini with sugar rim," she said and licked her lips. "Delicious."

The sight of her tongue on her plum-colored lips made his gut draw tight. "Noted. Favorite meal?"

"Depends on the day," she said. "Especially since I've been pregnant. Lately I've been craving macaroni and cheese," she said with a wince. "That's gonna do terrible things to my hips."

"Your hips are perfect. Favorite sandwich?" he continued.

"When I'm good, I'll take a chicken and vegetable wrap. When I'm bad, open-faced turkey with gravy and mashed potatoes or roast beef."

"I like that about you," he said, shooting her a smile. "I like that you are a red-meat eater," he said, remembering the way she'd once savored a steak with béarnaise sauce.

"Not lately," she said.

"Are you telling me you never want me to take you out for a steak?" he asked.

"No," she admitted. "Just later."

"Okay, I'll take a raincheck. Same for that strawberry martini," he said. "Favorite toy from childhood?"

She blinked. "My little pony," she said. "I always

wanted a pony, but I knew that was an impossible dream."

"Favorite dessert?" he continued, losing himself in her ocean-blue gaze.

"Chocolate anything," she said.

He smiled. "If you could travel anywhere, where would you go?"

"Europe."

"That's a whole continent," he said.

"And your point is?" she said, lifting her eyebrow.

He laughed, drinking in her audacity. "I wish my father had met you," he said.

"Why?" she asked. "I'm just an assistant."

He shook his head. "No, you're more. Observant, responsive and fascinating."

"Now, you flatter me," she said, flashing her eyes at him.

"Technically, I don't need to flatter you anymore. You married me, so I can coast."

"Oh, I think that would be a huge mistake," she said. "For both of us. Don't you?"

Seven

Brock made love to Elle through the night until she was too exhausted to continue. She curled up against his chest, slid her arms around his neck and fell asleep. The next morning she awoke to an empty place beside her. Elle lifted her head. She heard his voice, but not close by.

Pushing aside the covers, she rose from the bed and listened as she pulled on her robe. Was he downstairs? She crept closer to the bedroom door, and pushed it open.

"It's Sunday, for God's sake," Brock said, his voice carrying from downstairs. "Can't this wait?"

Silence followed. She heard Brock swear. "Okay, okay. I'll be back in town by this afternoon and in the office this evening." He swore again. "This better be worth it," he muttered.

Elle felt a twist in her stomach. The short, sweet time they'd shared together was over. Her chest hurt. Her heart hurt, but she didn't want him to feel bad after he'd made such an effort for them to get away. She bit her lip. "Hey," she called downstairs. "This has been wonderful, but I'm ready to return to civilization if you don't mind."

Brock walked out from under the second-floor landing so she could see him. Shirtless, he wore silk pants low on his hips. His bare chest was mesmerizing, his hair tousled by her fingers. He was the sexiest thing alive.

"You don't like the cabin?"

Her heart wrenched in her chest, but she forced herself to step up and give the response he needed. "No, I love it. But I have a ton to do and I'm starting to feel a little antsy," she said. "Do you mind?"

His gaze wrapped around hers for a long moment and he shook his head. "No," he said. "No problem. Let me know when you're ready. I'll load the car."

As soon as Elle and Brock arrived home in San Francisco, he returned to the office. Elle returned to redecorating the house. With the assistance of Bree, she'd found a decorator who helped her combine some of the older elements in the house with some of Brock's taste. Elle decided to retain a semi-formal tone for the living room and dining room for entertaining.

Brock was so busy he often didn't come to bed until after eleven o'clock, but he always rose early. She knew he was still feeling pressured by Golden Gate Promotions. Despite her grandfather's heart attack, he still hadn't given up his fight against Maddox. More than ever, Elle was aware of how much her deceit was costing Brock. It seemed as if all he did was work. She didn't see how they could possibly rebuild their relationship under the current circumstances, but she also couldn't exactly stomp her foot and demand he spend more time with her.

He surprised her one evening when he arrived home before dinner. She was eating a club sandwich in front of the television and debating whether to visit her mother again.

"Hey," he said, looking unbearably handsome in the doorway. "I like what you've done with the downstairs," he said. "You combined the old with the new and lightened it up." He glanced at her sandwich. "That looks good, too."

"I can fix you one," she said, standing, filled with the instant pleasure of just being with him.

He shook his head. "No, I can get the housekeeper. It won't take a—"

As if on cue, Anna stepped inside the room. "Good evening, Mr. Maddox. Mrs. Maddox." Glancing at Elle's plate, she shot her a disapproving glance. "Is there something I can get you?"

"I'll have the same thing she's having," Brock said. "With a beer."

"Club sandwich," Elle supplied with a sheepish smile.

"What was that about?" he asked curiously as he sat down beside her.

"Your staff gets really upset when I fix my own food. I think they consider it an insult," she said.

Brock chuckled. "Trust me, they're not used to anyone doing for themselves around here. Anna probably doesn't know what to do with you."

"How's work?" she asked, noticing that his lack of rest was visible around his eyes. "You look tired."

"You know I'm in the race for the gold against your grandfather. Can't take a lot of breaks."

Frustration filled her. "I don't understand him. I would have thought his heart condition would slow him down, or at least make him see reason."

"He and my father have a lot in common. My father was determined to leave the business for future generations of the Maddox family."

"Is that the way you feel?" she asked. "That you're building Maddox for your heirs?"

"At this point in the company's growth, it's more about taking care of the employees who are counting on me, and securing our growth for the future. I haven't spent a lot of time thinking about what my heir will ultimately do." Anna delivered the sandwich and beer. "Thank you," he said to her. "Why do you ask, Elle?"

"Just curious. Your father instilled in you a strong sense of family tradition and I wondered if you planned the same path for our child."

"You don't like that idea," he concluded, then shot her a sly smile. "You don't think I turned out well?"

"I didn't say that," she said, giving in to the urge to smile. "I just wouldn't want our child to feel locked in to only one choice."

"If it's a boy, he may want to play baseball," he said.

"Or sing opera," she said, choosing the polar opposite to watch Brock's reaction.

"Not if he gets my musical ability," Brock muttered, taking a bite of the sandwich and washing it down with a swig of beer. He let out a long sigh. "This is the most relaxed I've been since we left the mountain house. Thank God my dinner meeting had to cancel tonight."

Elle couldn't decide whether to feel offended or flattered. "Well, it's good to see you," she said. "I've missed you."

He glanced up and met her gaze for a long moment. "I can see how it would get lonely around here."

"It's not that," she said. "I was just used to seeing you at the office, so I spent most of my days with you."

He nodded. Something about him seemed restless, unsettled. "It won't always be this busy. I'll be around more."

"Will you really?" she asked, keeping her voice light even though her feelings were anything but. "That workaholic gene is pretty strong."

"You're not the first to notice," he said, his gaze turning moody. "After we get through this crisis, I want to shift things so that I can delegate more often. But in the meantime, you and I have received our first social invitation," he said, changing the subject. "Walter and Angela Prentice are having a cocktail party on Friday night and they specifically requested your presence."

The Prentice name was familiar to Elle—Walter's company was Maddox's most important client. "Do they know about the baby?" she asked, acutely aware that Walter was very image-conscious and wouldn't tolerate even a whiff of a scandal.

"I didn't mention it, but Walter's such a family man, I'm sure he'll be delighted with the news, since we're married."

"Family is everything," she said, repeating the Prentice slogan.

"Yes, it is," Brock said, taking a bite of his sandwich and leaning his head back against the sofa.

She felt a shot of sympathy for him, remembering the challenging days he'd endured when she'd worked for him. Finished with her dinner, she rose and stood behind him. "Take a deep breath and let the day go," she said, repeating what she'd told him in his apartment so many times.

"Hmm," he said as she sank her fingers into his shoulders.

"You can't work 24/7," she whispered. "You can't work right now, so you may as well rest. Rest and get stronger for when you *can* do something."

Brock inhaled and exhaled. "I remember how much I craved these massages at the end of the day," he murmured.

She gently rubbed his shoulder muscles with her thumb and forefinger. "Good?" she asked.

He groaned in response.

She continued to knead his shoulders as she brushed her mouth against his ear. "Does it feel good?"

"Yes," he said. "Too good. I want more," he continued. "I want to feel you every way I can. Inside and out," he said and turned around to meet her gaze. "Let's go upstairs."

"You haven't finished your sandwich," she said.

"I'm hungry for something else."

The next evening, Brock asked her to meet him at the Prentices' home, since he was running late. Elle dressed carefully, eager to convey just the right tone as

Brock's wife. After all, this was their first major public outing together. Fighting butterflies, she exited the car and climbed the steps to the Prentices' mansion.

With marble columns, a valet in the driveway and a man greeting guests in black tie at the door, the major clothing manufacturer's property oozed success, as it should.

"Good evening," the man at the door said. "Your name?"

"Elle Linton," she said, then corrected herself. "Elle Linton Maddox."

His gaze flicked over her in assessment and he nodded. "Welcome," he said and opened the door for her to enter.

Elle was immediately hit with the sights and sounds of an opulent party. The scents of gourmet food and wine filled the air. She heard a string quartet and smelled fresh-cut roses. Mirrors reflected guests dressed in couture fashions. She hoped the black gown with dark embroidered rosettes just below the bodice would pass muster. She brushed a strand of hair from her face and searched for Brock. She'd waited a few extra minutes to leave, not wanting to arrive before him.

A waiter offered her a glass of champagne and she shook her head. "No, thank you. Do you have water?"

He pointed to a waitress as the other end of the room where the chandeliers flashed light and brilliance that was reflected in the mirrors. "Thank you," she murmured, searching the crowd for Brock. She didn't see a soul she knew in the entire room, and wondered where the hosts were. She should at least be able to identify Walter Prentice since he had been in Brock's office before. Accepting a glass of water from the server, she nodded her thanks and backed against the wall. Perhaps she would be able to see Brock from here.

A group of men on one side of her discussed the terrible performance of the Giants. A group of women on her other side discussed plastic surgery. Elle caught fragments of each conversation.

"They need to trade the pitcher. He can't do anything," one man lamented.

"Have you heard about Dr. Frazier? He does amazing things with filler."

"If you ask me, it's not the pitcher, it's the management," another man said.

"I hear he worked on Carol Maddox. She looks a little too tight to me," a woman said.

Elle's ears perked up at the mention of her mother-in-law.

"She looks better now that he's plumped up her face a little. Speaking of Carol, did you hear about Brock? He's off the market," a woman said.

"Oh, no," several women murmured. "Who got him?"

"I hear he knocked up his assistant. The only reason he married her is because she's pregnant," the woman said.

Elle felt her face heat with embarrassment. Even though she knew the woman's words were true, the humiliation struck at the core of her. She wanted to defend her relationship with Brock. She wanted to tell the woman that she and Brock had experienced a closeness that neither of them had expected, yet both had cherished. But she wouldn't. Because the bottom line was, Elle had betrayed him and he'd married her because of the baby.

Taking a long drink of water, she strongly considered leaving. She could tell Brock she hadn't felt well...

"Well, well, Mrs. Maddox, what are you doing in the corner?" Walter Prentice said with a big smile and booming voice. "Come and meet my wife. She's been dying to see who finally slayed Brock Maddox and brought him to his knees."

Elle forced her lips into a smile and accepted the arm he offered. "Good evening, Mr. Prentice. You have a lovely home. And I wouldn't call it slayed," she said, referring to Brock. "I definitely didn't bring him to his knees."

"Oh, don't tell me Brock didn't give you a proper old-fashioned proposal?" he asked, ushering her through the crowd.

"Well, you know Brock. He's a breathtaking combination of tradition and cutting edge," she managed.

"Too true," he said. "Now, here's my wife, Angela. Angela, this is Brock's new bride, Elle."

The elegant woman gave her a warm, curious glance. "How lovely," she said. "Walter and I were so happy when we heard Brock had gotten married, although you two did a good job keeping it secret. Shame on you. Everyone loves a wedding."

"Brock wanted to keep it low-key. Neither of us expected our feelings to grow like they did," Elle said, working hard to keep the smile on her face.

"Brock has a good head on his shoulders," Walter said in approval. "Where is he?"

"I'm not sure," Elle said. "He was running a little late at the office. I'm certain he'll be here soon."

"He shouldn't keep his bride waiting," Mrs. Prentice said. "Let me introduce you to a few of my friends."

For the next half hour, Elle's head swam with new names. Mrs. Prentice, clearly an overachiever like her husband, introduced her to several people. When Mrs. Prentice emphasized the fact that Elle was Brock Maddox's new wife, Elle felt curious glances sizing her up. After fielding questions about their small wedding and nonexistent honeymoon, Elle managed to slip away to call Brock.

He picked up on the fifth ring. "Brock Maddox," he said curtly.

"Elle Linton Maddox," she returned just as curtly. "Where are you?" she asked. "The Prentices are asking for you."

"This cosmetics contract is a major headache," he said. "I'm running late."

"You said you were running late an hour and a half ago. What am I supposed to say to Mr. and Mrs. Prentice?"

"I'll leave now," he said. "See you in fifteen minutes."

He disconnected the call and Elle tucked her cell phone inside her evening bag. The house felt as if it were closing in on her. Desperately needing some fresh air, she walked outside to the patio where guests mingled, enjoying the beautiful night. She moved toward a column in a dark corner and sucked in the air. She looked up at the cloudy sky, shielding the stars, remembering a similar party that could have been a thousand years ago, or just yesterday.

Her grandfather had given permission for her to attend a Christmas party at his home. Elle had been eight years old and her mother had bought her a red velvet dress with lace at the hem and collar. Elle had been so excited. She'd hoped to meet her father, but he didn't show up. The other children had avoided her as if she were somehow less than them. The whole experience had been a disaster and she couldn't wait to get home and tear off her dress, put on her pajamas and go to bed. She remembered the feeling of not belonging all too well. She had the same feeling right now.

She stood there for several moments in the dark, wondering if she should leave, and if she did, whether anyone would notice. Then she heard a familiar male voice in the background.

"Walter, great to see you. You really know how to throw a party," Brock said as he walked within just a few feet of her. Her heart skittered at the sight of him.

"I met your wife earlier. She's beautiful. You shouldn't leave her on her own. Someone might steal her away," Walter said.

Brock gave a forced laugh. "You're right. Elle is beautiful. Do you know where she is?"

"I'm sure she's around here somewhere. The Missus was introducing her around," Mr. Prentice said. "I remember Elle was your assistant."

"Yes, she was," Brock said. "When I realized we had feelings for each other, I decided we should make our relationship official. I didn't want to muddy the professional waters."

"Good move," Walter said. "Keep business separate from romance. Congratulations again on your marriage."

"Thank you," Brock said. "Now, if you'll excuse me, I'd better go search for my bride."

Walter laughed and thumped Brock on the shoulder. "If anyone can find her, I'm sure it's you."

From the shadows, Elle watched as Brock pulled out his BlackBerry and sent a text message. Glancing around, he accepted a glass of wine from a server. He loosened his collar, looking impatient.

Elle wondered if she should step forward, but something kept her from it. Her wedding to Brock was all for show and she no longer knew if she could keep up the performance. Elle moved along the wall to the French doors and scooted through the crowd. All those years of being the Koteas's dirty little secret played through her mind, and here she was again, having been Brock's little secret. She felt like such a fraud. Brock didn't really want to be married to her. She couldn't help feeling like he resented her for the pregnancy.

Unable to bear the return of feelings she'd suffered since childhood, she dashed out the front door and asked the valet to hail a cab for her.

Although her mother didn't know the whole truth about her relationship with Brock, she did know Elle's history. She didn't know that Elle had accepted a deal with her grandfather to keep her mother well, but she knew just about everything else. Elle needed to see her.

"What a lovely surprise," Elle's mother said as she

rose from the sofa where she'd been watching television to greet her daughter. She studied Elle from head to toe. "You look lovely. What are you doing here?"

Elle flew into her mother's accepting arms. "What do you mean? Are you suggesting I usually look like a hag when I visit you?" Elle asked.

"Well, no," her mother said, pulling back slightly. "But you're not usually dressed to the nines. Want to tell me what this is about?"

"Can't we just enjoy the visit?" Elle begged.

"Hmm," her mother said doubtfully, dipping her head. "Sit down on the sofa and I'll pour you some green tea."

Elle made a face. "It smells like stinky socks," she said, but sat down, anyway.

"It's soothing," her mother retorted, heading for the kitchen, "and the antioxidants are good for both you and the baby."

Elle's cell phone rang and she frowned, fumbling in her small bag.

"Is that your cell I hear?" her mother asked.

Elle silenced her phone. "Oh, you're watching a Sandra Bullock movie. I miss our girls' nights together," she said.

Her mother reappeared with a cup of tea. "Who rang on your cell phone?"

"I'm not sure," Elle said, reaching for the tea. "It stopped."

"Uh-huh," her mother said and sat down beside her. "Elle, what's wrong? You know you can talk to me."

Elle's throat grew swollen with emotion. She'd carried so much during the last several months—the weight of her mother's illness, the deal with her grandfather, her secret affair with Brock and the pregnancy. And now, her misery over being married to a man who didn't love her.

"I just wanted to see you," Elle said. "I've been so busy I haven't had a chance to get over here during the last few days."

"Hmm," her mother said, but she slid her arm around Elle's shoulders and hugged her. Thank God for unconditional love. Elle felt the tears back up in her eyelids.

A knock sounded at the door.

Her mother turned, frowning. "Security didn't call. How odd."

Elle knew who it was. "Don't tell him I'm here."

Her mother stared at her. "Who?" she asked. "Elle, who?"

"Brock," Elle whispered and shook her head. "I just can't deal with him right now. I just can't."

Her mother sighed. "Elle, this is ridiculous. You can't hide from your husband."

"Please," Elle said.

"Is he abusing you?" her mother asked, grave concern on her face.

"Of course not," Elle said.

"Just a minute," her mother called and walked to the door. She opened it. "Hi, Brock. Elle and I were just talking about you."

Eight

"I searched for you at the party, but I couldn't find you," Brock said, looking at Elle. She was beautiful, dressed in a black, slinky gown that hid her pregnancy but accented her curves. Her eyes were smoky blue, her lips shiny and inviting. Her gaze, however, was cautious and guarded.

"I waited a long time, then I just followed a whim to visit my mother," Elle said, her smile forced, her eyes dark with secret emotions. He wondered what was going on.

"Prentice said he and his wife were happy to see you," he said.

"They were very gracious," she replied.

Brock wasn't quite sure how to approach Elle at this point. She clearly wasn't interested in seeing him. That was a first. When they'd been working together, she couldn't get enough of him. He'd felt the same for her. He still felt the same for her, although he didn't know when he would be able to fully trust her again. He had no doubt that she could sense that. Perhaps that was part of the problem.

He glanced at the television. "What are we watching?'

Elle's mother cleared her throat. "A Sandra Bullock movie," she said. "Would you like some green tea?"

Brock blinked. *Green tea?* He would rather drink dirty water. "Thank you," he said and sat down on the sofa. "I hear Sandra Bullock is up for an Oscar."

"Not for this movie," Elle's mother called as she walked toward the kitchen. "But she's my favorite actress."

"Why didn't you wait for me?" Brock asked Elle in a low voice.

"Do you have any idea how insulting it was to have to make excuses for you for almost two hours?" she said. "If you expect me to be a Stepford wife like your mother, you can forget it. We should just end it now."

"My mother," he echoed, appalled. "Why would I want you to be like my mother? Trust me, I have no oedipal urges. What happened at the party?" he asked gently. "Did something upset you?"

"Aside from waiting for you endlessly," Elle whispered, "I happened to overhear people say that the only reason you married me was because I was pregnant. Don't even try to deny it because we both know the truth."

Her desperation and vulnerability dug at him. "You and I both want the best for this baby," he said.

"Yes, but you and I need—" She stopped and lowered her voice. "You and I need to have a relationship," she whispered. "It can't all be about the baby or it's not going to work."

"We have never had a shortage of passion, Elle," he said.

"I want more than passion," she said. "I want compassion, companionship..." She took a deep breath. "I want love."

Brock felt his gut twist. "I can give you passion, compassion and companionship, but love is going to take a while. But I'll work at it. I promise," he said.

She stared at him with pain in her eyes. "I'm going to be blunt here. I don't want a marriage like your parents had."

Brock felt like she'd slapped him. "What the hell do you know about my parents' marriage? You've never even met my father," he said, a twinge of anger stinging a raw place inside him.

"You've obviously forgotten the earful your mother gave me," she said. "Besides, if you're a chip off the old block, then in a way, I *have* met your father."

"Here's the tea," Suzanne said as she brought Brock's cup to him, looking back and forth between Brock and Elle with concern. "It's still a little hot."

"Thank you," he said.

"This is...nice," she said, sitting down without taking her eyes off them. "Enjoying a movie with my daughter and son-in-law. Shall we watch the rest?"

Brock only made it through the chick flick because he was so distracted by what was happening with Elle that he could barely follow what was on screen. What had gotten into her? He'd thought she would be excited about attending the Prentices' cocktail party.

The interminable movie finally ended and Brock rose to his feet. "Time to go. Elle needs her rest and so do you," he said to his mother-in-law.

"How thoughtful," Suzanne said, taking his hand and looking directly in his eyes. "I'm so glad you're looking after Elle."

"I wouldn't have it any other way," he said to reassure her. "Thank you for your hospitality, Suzanne. Ready, Elle?"

Elle met his gaze with a hint of a mutinous expression that didn't bode well for the ride home. He could feel the chill already. "Yes," she finally said and gave her mother a hug. "I'll talk to you soon," she promised and joined Brock as they left the condo.

They walked to his car in silence and Brock ushered her into the passenger seat of his Porsche. He rounded the vehicle, slid in and started the engine. "I think we should start this conversation over. First, I apologize for being late tonight. This prospective cosmetics account is almost more demanding than the Prentice account."

Glancing at her, he noticed her arms were crossed firmly and her jaw was set. But after a long silence, she finally gave a heavy sigh. "Apology accepted. In the future, however, I would appreciate it if you would keep me better informed about delays."

He nodded. "I can do that. Now, about us…it's going to take time, Elle," he said.

"Exactly. With the schedule you keep at the office, it's going to be difficult for you to put in any time on our marriage."

Brock had heard something similar from his ex-fiancée just before she'd left him. His gut tightened at the prospect of Elle doing the same. He'd hoped that since she'd been his assistant, she would understand his devotion to the company. He'd also hoped that because of all the nights they'd shared, she would somehow know, deep down, that his drive for his company was part of his blood, part of his very being.

"Are you complaining about my work hours?" he asked.

She narrowed her eyes. "I resent that. I'm not complaining. But let's look at this a different way. If you were trying to build a business relationship with me, how much time would you put in?"

He blinked at her challenge.

"I'll take a wild guess and say you might want my relationship with you to last at least as long as your relationship with Prentice," she said.

He took a deep breath as he pulled into the driveway. "Of course I want our marriage to last," he muttered. He parked in the garage and turned to her. "What are you trying to say?"

"It's easy," she said. "If we both want our relationship to work, we both need to put in the time."

"We spend every night together," he said.

"Asleep," she said.

"We don't sleep for the first two hours."

She let out a quick breath. "We need to be about more than sex," she whispered, her eyes dark and tumultuous.

"Are you saying I don't satisfy you?" he demanded.

She bit her lip. "I'm not saying that, but maybe we

should put the emphasis in our relationship on something else," she said. "For a while."

"You want to date," he concluded, incredulous. But when he gave it some thought, it made sense.

She licked her lips and he felt himself grow hard. He had felt that mouth against his, sliding down his throat and chest, down lower, taking him to insane heights....

"We never did that, Brock," she said. "We never just...dated."

"Okay," he said slowly. "Does that mean we sleep together or not?"

"That's up to you," she said. "If we waited for a little while to—" She broke off. "Do you still want to sleep together while we figure this out?"

Brock decided to leave the ball in her court, since this was her idea. "I'll let you decide," he said, rising from the car and crossing over to open the passenger door. "Dinner tomorrow night?"

"I'd rather hike on Sunday," she said.

Brock swallowed.

"Is that okay?" she asked.

"Sure," he said. He could last. He'd suffered far worse than unmet sexual need in his life.

Less than an hour later, Brock slid into bed and Elle curled against him. "Thank you," she whispered, her lips against the back of his neck. He felt her breasts against him, her hand over his abdomen. He wondered if he would be able to stand this all night long.

Brock took a deep breath. He'd grown accustomed to making love to Elle every night. After all, she was his wife. She stirred his passions and was incredibly responsive. Why should he deny himself? Or her?

He knew, however, that she wanted him to use some restraint. It would take every bit of his determination, but he would damn well do it. Elle was worth it. And so was their marriage.

Sunday afternoon, Elle climbed up a trail behind Brock. She inhaled deeply, disgusted with her lack of physical fitness.

"You okay?" Brock asked, looking over his shoulder.

"Sure," she said breathlessly.

He turned around and came to a stop. "You don't sound okay," he said, searching her face.

She put her hands on her hips as she tried to catch her breath. "It's the altitude," she said.

He grinned. "Not the exertion?"

She scowled at him. "The climb has been straight up."

"I thought you could handle it," he said.

"I can," she replied and took a deep breath.

His blue eyes flickered over her. "Let's take a break and drink some water."

"You're just saying that because I'm pregnant," she said.

"I'm thirsty," he said, sitting down as he pulled out his bottle of water. "Aren't you?"

Elle sank onto a rock and also pulled out her water. She drank down the cool liquid quickly.

"You should make sure to keep hydrated," Brock said.

"I will," she said, downing almost all of the bottle.

"Want mine?" he asked.

"No, I'm good," she said.

He pulled an extra bottle from his backpack and offered it to her. "I want to make sure my wife and baby have plenty of water."

She finished hers and accepted his. "Thanks from both of us."

He enclosed her hand in his. "Let's go back down," he said.

"I feel a little like a wimp. I didn't expect to get this tired this soon."

"You're pregnant," Brock said. "You're feeding and breathing and doing everything for two."

Elle couldn't resist smiling. "Thanks," she said, drawing strength from the clasp of his hand. "Let's go back down."

"Good. Now tell me, when you were a little girl, what did you want for Christmas?"

Elle did a double take. "For Christmas? A father," she said, unable to keep the words from escaping her mouth.

Brock stopped midstep. "A father," he echoed. "I'll always be a father to our child," he promised.

"Will you show up at most of his soccer games or her ballet recitals?" she asked.

He took a quick breath. "Yes, I will."

She nodded and started to walk again. "That's good," she said, making her way down the trail.

"When you were a little girl," Brock said, "what kind of husband did you want?"

"I dreamed of Prince Charming sweeping me away to a fairytale kingdom with a huge castle with housekeepers and cooks. But I was in charge of the babies," she said. "We didn't have nannies because the prince and I took care of our children."

Her childhood dream moved him.

"Crazy, isn't it?" Elle said.

Brock pulled her against him. "Not crazy at all."

As they made their way down the last part of the path, Brock asked half a dozen more questions.

"What are your favorite movies?" he asked.

"I hate to say it," she said.

"Sandra Bullock movies," he said.

"Yes, and Julia Roberts. I like girl-power movies. Comes from being left in the shadow of my father and grandfather," she said.

"Understandable," Brock said. "Your favorite flower is the rose. And you especially love a multicolored arrangement."

She stared at him in surprise. "How did you know that?"

"I got you flowers a few times. I caught you smelling the roses more than once."

"I didn't know you'd noticed," she said, meeting his gaze.

"I didn't notice as much as I should have," he said. "But I noticed a few things. I'll notice more in the future," he promised.

She rested her forehead against his. "What's your favorite flower?"

Surprise rushed through him. "I've never thought about it."

"Think about it," she said, smiling.

He shrugged his shoulders. "I don't know. Wild flowers?"

"Hmm. I'm not so sure about that."

"You're not going to argue with me about my favorite flower, are you?" he challenged.

Elle sighed. "Okay," she relented. "So which sports event are you dying to attend?"

He laughed. "Lots of them, but I can't make time for them all," he said. "Would you go with me?"

"Of course."

"Good," he said, pulling her into a hug and sliding his hands down over her butt, lifting her against him. "You never quit making me want you," he said.

Elle brushed her lips over his. "Who, me?"

"Oh, yeah," he said. "You."

That night as she snuggled in his arms, Brock wanted her more than ever. His need for her alarmed him, but the sensation of her skin against his and her clean, sexy scent distracted him. He resigned himself to another night of frustration and forced his eyes closed.

Seconds later, he felt her hand drift over his chest, down to his abdomen. He caught that wicked, curious hand just before she touched him where he was hard and wanting her. "No teasing," he said in a low voice.

She lifted her lips to his, her eyelids fluttering to a sultry half-mast. "What if the teasing will be followed by satisfaction?"

"I thought you wanted us to take some time—"

She rubbed her mouth against his, sliding her tongue just inside. "I want you, too, Brock," she confessed. "It's hard for me to stay away from you."

"If you're sure," he said, loosening his grip on her

hand. Two breaths later she was touching him intimately and kissing him as if there was no tomorrow. He wondered if he would ever get enough of her.

They made love that night and when Brock awakened in the morning, he was caught between wanting to take her again and giving her a break. He wanted Elle too much. She got under his skin.

The following week, despite their discussion, Brock came home late every night. Elle refused to be a nag. She occupied herself by visiting her mother and grandfather, and continuing with redecorating the house. On Friday, Brock left before she rose, but Elle decided to take breakfast in the sunroom, anyway.

Yawning, she indulged in eggs, bacon and blueberry pancakes. The housekeeper brought her the newspaper and she scanned it as she ate. Just as she was finishing a gooey, delicious bite of pancake, she glimpsed a photo of Brock with a beautiful blonde. He was lifting a glass of wine and she was laughing

Elle's food lodged in her throat. "Oh, my God," she said, choking, coughing then swallowing. She read the caption beneath the photo. "Hot San Francisco Mad Man Brock Maddox charms cosmetics queen Lenora Hudgins."

Elle stared at the photo, absorbing every detail. Lenora was beautiful. Brock looked charming and sexy. She wanted to club him. She was staying home every night when he was out *courting* Lenora Hudgins. Or her account, anyway.

Twelve hours later, she was still steaming as she waited for Brock to return home. He finally wandered in at eight o'clock as she finished a BLT while watching her second Julia Roberts movie. Taking a deep breath, she focused on that big-screen TV instead of how furious she was with her husband.

"Julia Roberts," he said. "Did she win an Oscar for this one?"

"No. I watched that one earlier," she said.

Silence stretched between them. "How was your day?" he asked.

"Downhill after my second blueberry pancake," she said, "thanks to your photo with Lenora in the paper."

Another silence fell like a lead weight. "What photo?"

"The one in the paper this morning," she said, still not looking at him. "You didn't see it?"

He swore. "No. I didn't. You didn't read anything into that photo, did you?" he asked. "Because it was all business."

"Hmm," she said. "If I were the jealous type, I would have to disagree. I can't help wondering how you would feel if the roles were reversed and I were toasting a man with that kind of smile on my face." She thrust the paper toward him, her gaze focused on Julia Roberts on the screen. "You want to answer that one?"

"It isn't what it looks like, Elle. Come on. You worked for me. You know exactly what those dinners are all about."

"Again, how would you respond if that were me in the photo? And I said 'it isn't what it looks like?'" she asked.

"I would want to beat the guy to a pulp," he conceded.

She finally met his gaze. "I don't think Lenora would look good with a black eye," she said. "I also don't think you would get the account if I punched her."

"You want to join me the next time Lenora and I have dinner?" he asked.

"I think you might have a hard time winning the account with your pregnant wife along," she said.

"You didn't answer my question."

"Any chance I can get some free makeup samples?" she asked.

His lips twitched. "What do you want me to do?"

"Tell me how much she turns you off," she said.

"She does," Brock said. "Plastic. Over-Botoxed. Her skin is so tightly stretched she looks like she's permanently in a spaceship with a G-force blowing back her skin."

"You're exaggerating," she said.

He chuckled. "The woman is impossible to please. She's an alien."

"Does she want you to go to bed with her?"

"No, Elle, she's just incredibly difficult and demands a lot of attention," he said, irritation bleeding through his cool countenance.

His response aroused her curiosity. "In what way?"

"Do you really want to know?" he asked.

"Yes, I do. I miss the activity at the office. Hearing about your work is fun for me," she said and he sat down beside her. "Tell me about her. Is she married? Does she have children? How old is she?"

"Unmarried, one child, college-aged, she's fifty-three. She's had too many face-lifts and works out too much," he said.

"Scared, but gotta be tough to stay on top," Elle said. "Bring her here for dinner one night next week. We'll have roast chicken, mashed potatoes, string beans and biscuits."

"The only thing she'll eat is the chicken," he said.

"We'll see," she said.

He narrowed his eyes at her. "What makes you so sure?"

"What have you got to lose?" she countered.

He shrugged. "Good point."

They slept together for the next three nights, but didn't make love, even though their experiment was technically over. The lack of intimacy relieved Elle, then made her feel uneasy. She tried not to focus on it. On Monday night, Lenora was scheduled to arrive for dinner at six. By six-thirty, she still hadn't arrived.

"This is why I can't stand dealing with this woman," Brock muttered, pacing from one end of the den to the other.

Five minutes later, the doorbell rang. "I can't believe it," he said. "She finally showed."

Elle allowed the housekeeper to greet Lenora, then counted to ten and rose. She slid her hand inside Brock's and walked toward the dining room. He squeezed her hand and glanced at her. "Thanks," he muttered.

Lenora swept into the hallway. "I'm so sorry I'm late. Crazy Monday," the platinum blonde with smoky eyes and a too-thin frame said.

"Lenora, we're glad you could come. This is my wife, Elle."

"Nice to meet you, Elle. Something smells delicious."

"Just a little home cooking. I figure a hardworking woman could use a little home cooking every now and then," Elle said.

Lenora studied her for a moment, then sighed. "Comfort food," she said. "I never indulge, but I just might tonight."

"It won't hurt you," Elle said. "As my mother would say, you could use some fattening up. Come into the dining room. You've earned your dinner."

Lenora smiled. "I'll pay with the elliptical tomorrow, but you're tempting me."

"We all gotta live," Elle said, and the three of them entered the dining room.

After Lenora consumed chicken, mashed potatoes, stuffing, biscuits and green beans, she groaned as she sat back in her chair. "That was delicious. So bad, but so good."

"Give yourself a break," Elle said. "You obviously work like a dog."

"I like her," Lenora said to Brock. "Where did you find her?"

"In my office," Brock said. "I got lucky."

"So you did," Lenora said, one of her over-Botoxed eyebrows rising just slightly. "Tell me, Elle, how do you plan to approach aging?" she asked. "Not that you're anywhere near it."

Elle sighed. "I'm conflicted. I want to take care of my skin, but you know, Catherine Deneuve doesn't believe in staying too thin. We women have a tough road to hoe, but I don't think I want to kill myself after forty-five. I mean, the truth is, no one is paying me to look good."

Lenora gave a short laugh. "So true. So your theory is to look good without overextending yourself. Make it as easy as possible," the woman said.

"The kiss method," Elle said. "Keep it simple, sweetheart."

"Ooh," Lenora said. "I like that." She clasped her fingers together and leaned forward. "Okay, Mr. Maddox, I want to sign with your company. And our campaign will be 'Keep It Simple, Sweetheart.' It works for any age, from teens to young twenties to new moms to women of a certain age."

Brock shot Elle a cryptic smile. "I couldn't agree more."

Three hours later, after everyone—including Lenora—ate a slice of hot apple pie à la mode, Brock led Elle to bed. "I've missed you in the office," he said, taking her clothes off.

She felt her heart beat faster. "Are you ready to trust me again?" she asked.

"You did get me a new account tonight. Maybe I should hire you as a copy writer," he said, grinning. "Did I remove your fears about any possibility of attraction to Lenora?"

"I thought she was lovely," she said, lifting her hands to sift through his hair.

"She's a barracuda," he said. "You're very sharp, but you're also compassionate. I've always been drawn to you for those qualities."

"Hmm," she said, enjoying the way his hands slid over her skin.

"You are irresistibly sexy. I can't get enough of you," he said, skimming his hands over her belly. "Hey, Elle, I owe you one. You really did land me that new account, you know. She wasn't convinced until she met you."

His acknowledgement made her stomach twist. "Take it out in trade," she whispered. "For what happened with my grand—"

His mouth covered hers, keeping her from finishing the word. "In the past," he said, sliding one of his hands over her swollen breast.

She savored the sensation of his mouth on hers. "I want to please you," she said, even though what she really wanted to say was *I love you*. But she couldn't say that. Not yet.

"You do," Brock said.

"How?" she asked.

"Just by being here with me," he said.

The following Sunday was Father's Day. The day was always rough for Brock. Even though his father often had been out of town, the two of them had always talked on the phone. Brock would say how lucky he was and his father would laugh, but his gratitude and pride had been clear.

Since his father had died, Brock spent Father's Day remembering his dad. Staring out the window as he sipped a cup of coffee, he felt Elle come up behind him and wrap her arms around him. Something inside him eased. He covered her hands with his.

"What are you thinking about?" she whispered.

He inhaled deeply. "My dad," he said.

Silence stretched between them for several seconds. "Father's Day," she said.

"Yeah," he said, nodding.

"Do you have good memories of how your father spent the day with you and your brother?" she asked.

"Not really," Brock said. "But we always touched base by phone. I miss being able to give him a call."

"Hmm. Understandable." She gave him a squeeze. "I spent every Father's Day indulging in fantasies about how a father would teach me to pitch and catch. Or swing a bat. Or play golf. Or read the Sunday cartoons. Or just tell me super-wise things about life."

"Your father missed out by not getting to know you," Brock said, turning toward her.

"I missed out, too," she said.

"Have you ever met him?" he asked.

She shook her head. "He moved to Chicago and never came back. My grandfather stepped in to give my mother and me financial support, but—" She shrugged. "I was more of an irritation and burden than anything else."

"Irritation," he repeated, sliding his finger over her jawline. "You know that pearls are created by the irritation of a grain of sand."

"I've never been called a pearl before," she said.

"Can't imagine why," he said, rubbing his hands over her shoulders. "Seems obvious to me."

She smiled. "You're a charmer."

He shook his head. "I'm just calling it the way I see it."

"I have a small gift for you," she said.

"Why?" he asked.

"For Father's Day," she said.

"I'm not a father yet."

"Close enough," she said. "Check out your Black-Berry."

The smile on her face jacked up his curiosity. "What have you been up to?"

Her smile grew wider. "Don't ask me. Check it out for yourself."

Brock went to his phone charger and picked up the BlackBerry. Noticing there was a message, he pushed the button.

"Turn up the sound," she said.

He listened as a disco tune began to play and the ultrasound image of his child danced across the tiny screen. He felt joy shoot through him. "Look at him move," he said. "Or her." He watched, amazed at the sight of the tiny little combination of him and Elle. Unable to resist, he played the video again, staring at his dancing baby. When it ended, he played it again.

Elle gave a soft, throaty giggle. "You like it," she said.

He met her gaze. "I do."

"Here's your Father's Day card," she said, handing him an envelope.

Feeling a strange dip in his gut, he tore open the envelope and read the card. As he read, it hit him hard that his life was changing. Moved, he stared at the card and wondered if his mother had ever given his father such a card. And if she had, Brock wondered if his father had cared. He'd known his father wasn't particularly emotional. James Maddox had been determined to build the most successful advertising agency in San Francisco.

James Maddox had also wanted a beautiful wife. James Maddox had also wanted children. James Maddox got what he wanted.

He'd been a demanding man. At times, Brock had sweated meeting those high standards. He knew his brother had struggled with those standards, soared past them, and flipped the bird at them. Brock actually admired his brother for that.

As much as Brock had revered his father, he'd never felt close to him. Did he want that same kind of relationship with his own child? Brock frowned.

"What is it?"

"Just thinking," he muttered.

"About?" she asked, lifting her hand to his cheek.

"Being a father. Figuring out what kind of father I need to be," he said. "Different than the dad you didn't have. Different than the father I did have."

Elle swallowed audibly. "You're going to be amazing," she said, her eyes shiny with unshed tears.

"How can you be so sure?" he asked.

"I know you have an amazing mind and incredible drive. But I also know something a lot of other people don't know. You, Brock Maddox, have an awesome heart."

Nine

As Brock reviewed some new copy for the Prentice campaign, his intercom buzzed. "Yes?"

"Flynn Maddox is here," his assistant said.

Brock smiled. "Send him in."

Flynn burst through the door. "How's married life?"

"I could ask you the same," Brock said, standing and slapping his brother on the back.

"Couldn't be better," Flynn said. "I just want to thank you again for keeping those divorce papers out of my hands all those years ago."

"Your marital problems were partly my fault. I realized that," he said. "I'm glad you're happy now."

"Happy as a clam," he said. "How about you?"

Brock nodded. "It's going as well as it could."

Flynn rocked back on his heels and studied him. "Could be better?"

"I didn't expect to feel this much for her. I don't know how to handle it. Every time I try to guard my feelings, she finds a different way in."

Flynn's lips lifted in a half grin. "I like this. The woman has knocked my rock-solid brother off balance."

Brock swore at him.

Flynn chuckled, then his smile fell and he shook his head. "You're not sure about her because of her grandfather, right?"

"Wouldn't you wonder the same?" Brock asked, pacing to the other side of his office. His doubts made him feel like a caged animal.

"Now, with Renee?" Flynn asked. "No. It sounds corny, but love is rare. You shouldn't fight it, or you could miss your chance forever."

Brock felt a lump of emotion in his throat. "How did you let go?"

"After I lost Renee the first time, I knew I had to do everything I could to keep her when I got her back. But you don't always get a second chance. And it's not easy. If you need proof, look at Renee and me. Even though Mother has done her best to keep us apart, we've managed to overcome her this time."

"You're right about Mother," Brock said. "She tried to poison Elle against me. I decided she needed to live somewhere else. I paid for a new place for her."

Flynn whistled. "I'm sure that wasn't cheap."

"It was necessary," Brock said. "She's a bored and

unhappy woman. I just wish she would find a wealthy husband who would take her away and occupy her."

"You and me both," Flynn said. "You and me both."

When Brock was forced to work through the weekend on a project for Prentice, Elle decided to take action. Picnic basket in hand, she walked into Maddox Communications and smiled at the security guard. "Elle Maddox. I'm going up to see my husband," she said, pointing to her basket. "I want it to be a surprise."

"May I see your ID?" the man at the desk asked.

His request gave her pause, but she pulled out her driver's license. "Here it is," she said and smiled.

The man checked a list. "Wait just a second please," he said, picking up his phone as he stepped away.

Curious, she watched as he spoke on the phone. What was this about?

The security man returned and nodded to her. "If you'll wait just a couple moments," he said.

Her stomach tightened. "Isn't my name on the approved list?" she asked.

"Just a moment," he said, clearly hedging his response.

The elevator doors opened and Logan Emerson entered the foyer. He met Elle's gaze as he walked toward her. "Mrs. Maddox," he said with a nod. "How are you tonight?"

"I'm fine," Elle said, recognizing the man who had caught her in the worst deception of her life. She couldn't blame him, and yet at the same she couldn't stop the heat of humiliation. "How are you?"

"Fine," he said, glancing at the basket she held in her hand. "Dinner?"

"A surprise for my husband," she said.

He nodded again. "Mind if I look?" he asked. "It's been a long time since I've had a home-cooked meal."

She didn't believe him for a second but she opened the basket. "Roast beef sandwiches with cheese and just a hint of horseradish on whole wheat of course, so we can pretend it's healthy. Whole wheat pasta with sundried tomatoes and pesto. And chocolate pie with whipped cream."

Logan winced. "Ouch. When was the last time I had homemade chocolate pie with whipped cream?"

"Do you want mine?"

"Is that a bribe?"

She narrowed her eyes in anger and lifted her chin. "You son of a bitch," she said. "If you haven't changed every computer code and key in that office, then you're not worth your fee. And I *will* tell Brock the same thing. I'm just here to see my husband for dinner," she said in a low voice, more desperate than she'd intended.

Logan held her gaze for a long moment. "I guess this means I'm not getting any of that chocolate pie," he said.

"You guess correctly."

"It's my job to protect Maddox and Brock," Logan said.

"You keep doing that," Elle said. "And it's my job to look after Brock and our marriage. Frankly," she said, lowering her voice, "I'm glad you caught me."

He blinked, a flicker of emotion flashing through his

eyes before his expression became inscrutable. "She's cleared," Logan said to the security guard.

"Just for tonight?" the guard asked.

"For anytime," Logan said. "Any questions from anyone, ask me." Logan turned to the elevator and swiped his card. Then he extended his hand. "Mrs. Maddox, your husband is hunched over his desk. He needs a break."

Feeling a strange combination of triumph and gratitude, she walked toward the elevator. She stopped just before she stepped into it. Sighing, she pulled out one of the pieces of pie and gave it to Logan. "No obligation. No payback. No bribe," she said. "Enjoy it and find a woman who will bake a pie for you every now and then."

She walked into the elevator and punched the button for Brock's apartment. Gripping the basket tightly, she counted the floors as she rose. Finally, she arrived on Brock's private floor and tiptoed into the darkened suite. She and Brock had spent so much time here. She smiled as she remembered sharing Chinese takeout, laughter and amazing sex. She remembered holding him and feeling him relax in her arms. Brock was always so tense; it gave her such pleasure that he could actually feel at ease enough with her that he could rest.

Tonight, she hoped she could help him the same way she once had. The room was actually a bit chilly. She glanced around, glimpsing a fine layer of dust and smelling the faint scent of mustiness. "Oh, my goodness," she murmured and turned on the light.

If she didn't know better, she would suspect that no one had been here since the last time she and Brock had shared a night together. That couldn't be possible, she told herself. She slid her finger through the dust on a table against the wall and walked toward the bedroom. The large bed was neatly made, the bedside tables empty. She walked into the bathroom and there was nothing on the counter. She rubbed her fingers over the bristles of the toothbrush. They were dry.

Elle couldn't deny the fact that the clear evidence of Brock's absence comforted her terrified heart. She hated the idea that he might have replaced her. Every indication suggested that he hadn't.

She pulled the bottle of red wine from the basket and poured it in a glass she pulled from the cabinet. Inhaling deeply, she savored the bouquet of the wine and then poured herself a glass of sparkling water the chef had packed for her. She pulled several candles from a different cabinet and lit them. After she set out the picnic, she took the backstairs to Brock's office and knocked on his closed door.

No response. She knocked again.

"Hello?" Brock's voice said from the other side of the door. "Who is it?"

"Your evil wife," she said.

The door immediately opened and Brock stared her, his shirt loosened, his tie discarded, his expression stunned. "What are you doing here?"

"Dinner," she said and kissed his cheek.

"Where?" he asked, looking at her empty hands.

"Upstairs," she said and smiled. "If you can spare a few minutes."

Brock met her gaze and his lids lowered in sexual

response. "I haven't been to my apartment since the last time you and I were together," he said.

"I know," she said. "Time we changed that, don't you think?"

He took her hand and slid his fingers through hers. "Sounds good to me."

She led him up the back stairs to the apartment where she'd left candles glowing in the darkness.

"Nice," he said.

"It gets better," she said and led him to the low table in the small den where they'd shared so many meals before.

"What made you do this?" he asked as he lowered himself to the floor.

She followed him to a sitting position. "You've been burning the midnight oil too much lately."

"Just one night," he said, reaching for his sandwich. "Oh, my favorite."

"Try three nights," she corrected.

"That long?" he said, surprised. He took a bite. "This is heaven. Oh, and pasta salad." He took a long sip of red wine and sighed. "You are my dream come true."

"Anyone could have brought you a roast beef sandwich with horseradish, pasta salad and red wine," she said.

He shook his head. "Nobody but you could be sitting across from me. Nobody," he said, "but you."

"How can I resist that?" she asked.

"I damn well hope you can't," he said and chomped through the rest of his sandwich, washing it down with wine. "How's the bedroom?"

She shot him a demure look. "How would I know?"

"Are you saying you don't know?" he demanded, pouring more wine into his glass.

"I think the bed needs to be exercised," she said, sipping from her own glass.

"Any chance you'll exercise the bed with me?"

She leaned across the table and pressed her mouth to his. "I thought you'd never ask."

As dawn broke through the curtains the next morning, Brock struggled to bring himself to a wakeful state. He fluttered his eyes open and tried to focus. Groaning, he started to get up.

He felt Elle slide her hand over his waist to his abdomen.

"It's too early," she whispered.

"Can't argue with that," he said and turned toward her, pulling her warm, sexy body against his. "I can't decide if it's totally bad or totally good that you came to see me at the office."

She ran her fingers through his hair. "You better say it's totally good," she said.

He chuckled and slid his hands down her waist to her bottom to pull her against him. "Totally good," he said and groaned as he felt himself grow hard. He swore under his breath.

She rubbed her sweet lips against his mouth and wriggled her honey-soft nether regions against him where he was hard and already wanting. "Oh, Elle, I can't get enough of you."

He pulled her against him and slid against her wetness, seeking, wanting, needing. He found her swollen opening and thrust inside her.

She gasped and the sound aroused him even more.

"Brock," she whispered. "I need you."

"You've got me," he promised, thrusting inside her. "In every way."

She enclosed him with her wet velvet, gasping and begging. The sound of her breath and voice made him crazy. He craved her with every inch of his being. The sensation of her silken warmth drove him over the edge. With just another thrust, he felt his climax roar through him, sending him into a spasm of pleasure.

"Elle," he whispered, sinking down on her.

"Oh, yes," she said, clinging to him. She rubbed her lips over his ear. "This almost makes me want to move into this apartment."

A chuckle rumbled up from his gut. "I'd never get any work done."

"You did before," she said.

"That was tough. You were a major distraction. I couldn't wait for the end of the day when you and I would escape," he said. "Now that you're pregnant and you're my wife, it's just as strong as ever."

"Really?" she asked, her gaze puzzled as she stared up at him. "You don't seem to have a problem coming home late."

"The company's in a transition period. That will change," he said. He was trying to put the pressure on Golden Gate, but he couldn't tell Elle about it. He wanted to, but she was too close to the situation emotionally. He knew she felt some tug of gratitude toward her grandfather. The knowledge dug at him, but soon enough, he would remove that obstacle between them.

She gave a sigh. "Until then, I guess I'll have to rescue you every once in a while."

"Rescue me?" he echoed, wondering what she meant.

"From work," she said. "I'll bring you a meal and use it to lure you up to your office apartment. And then who knows what else will happen?" she said, grinning up at him.

That day, as Elle began work on a picture display for Brock in the sunroom, the doorbell rang and Anna appeared. "Mrs. Maddox is here."

Elle lifted her eyebrows. "Which one?" she asked, hoping it was Renee.

"Oh, I'm sorry. Mrs. Carol Maddox," the housekeeper said.

"Oh, there you are," Carol said, coming from the hallway. She smiled at the housekeeper. "No need for formal announcements. We're family here. You've made a lot of changes in a short amount of time. The house has a more sparse feel to it," Carol said. "How does Brock like it?"

"Very much. I'm trying to create a combination of new and traditional. Bree has helped me," Elle said.

"I didn't know she was an interior designer," Carol said.

"She has an amazing eye," Elle replied.

Carol stepped closer and studied the photo display. "What's this?"

"A surprise for Brock. I know his memories of his father are important to him, so I wanted to display them in a meaningful way."

"Oh, look, there are even a few of me in there," she said with a bite in her tone. "At the hospital and at Brock's graduation. Don't mind me. I'm just the mother," she said and gave a brittle laugh.

"The focus of the subject is Brock's father. I see it as a memorial of the best of him," she said.

"That will be a challenge," Carol murmured. "But that's not the reason I came. I realize it's last-minute, but I, too, have been hard at work on my new home. Of course, it will never be as large or as impressive as this, but I like to think I've turned it into a stylish place. I'm having a little housewarming tomorrow night from seven to nine, and I insist that you and Brock join me."

Elle blinked. "Tomorrow night?"

"I can't believe you're booked. I know Brock has only made one public appearance with you, so—"

Elle felt the stab of shame. Carol was insinuating that Brock was embarrassed by her, embarrassed that he'd married her. "I'll have to ask him. He's been swamped at work."

Carol shot her a sympathetic but knowing gaze. "As he always will be. Do try to drag him away for just a little while tomorrow night. I'd like him to see my new residence. It would be embarrassing to me if he didn't attend. I'm counting on you," she said and smiled. "Good luck on the photo memorial. Such a sweet gesture. Ta-ta for now."

Elle broke the news about his mother's "invitation" when Brock finally arrived home that night and was eating a late dinner.

He paused, midbite. "You've got to be kidding. Of

all the ways I want to spend my nonexistent spare time, that is not one of them."

"I know," she said. "But she's your mother and it's not as if we'll have to stay the entire time."

He clenched his jaw. "Nothing good ever comes of being with her."

Elle laughed under her breath. "You can't say that. After all, your father created you and Flynn by being with her."

Brock rolled his eyes. "Well, since then," he amended. "I don't understand why you're taking her side on this."

Elle shrugged. "It's not a side. She's your mother, your only living parent."

Brock was silent for a long moment. "It makes you think about your mother and her health issues."

"I don't want you to have regrets," Elle said. "Your mother may be a pain in the butt, however, she did give birth to you. And who knows what really went on between your father and mother? Even you've said he took her for granted."

"Okay, we'll go for a half hour," he said.

Elle nodded, thinking about the little stabs Carol had taken at her during their conversation.

"You're too quiet," Brock said, studying her.

She took a sip of sparkling water, not wanting to reveal her insecurities.

"What is it?" he demanded. "What else did she say?"

"She wasn't here that long," Elle said.

"Long enough to cause trouble. What else did she say?"

Feeling pinned against the wall, Elle lifted her

shoulders. "She just made a point of saying that you and I hadn't made but one public appearance. I was probably reading something into it."

"Such as?" he asked.

"That you're embarrassed by me," she said and bit her lip.

Brock rolled his eyes. "You've got to be kidding."

"Well, you have to admit we married quickly. And I'm pregnant. And I used to be your assistant. These are all the kinds of things that make for conversation," she said.

"Gossip, you mean," he corrected. "The reason I've turned down invitations was to give us a chance to get used to the idea of being married. I especially didn't want you to have any additional pressure. You've gone through enough during the last few months."

"So, you're not ashamed of me?" she asked.

He shook his head. "Just very protective."

A ripple of pleasure and excitement raced through her at the hard expression on his face. Elle had never had a man in her life so determined to protect her, and it was something she'd secretly longed for as long as she could remember. Brock's devotion touched a core part of her and she wondered how much longer she would be able to keep herself from expressing her love for him. And when she did, would it be a treasure or burden?

Elle dressed carefully as she prepared for her mother-in-law's housewarming. She didn't want to feel self-conscious, but she had a feeling that nothing she wore was going to change that. She fixed her hair for the third time and dabbed on some lip gloss.

"You look beautiful," Brock said from the doorway. "Can we get this over with?"

Elle smothered a laugh at his impatience. "Thank you and yes," she said, walking toward him.

She liked the way her blue silk dress flowed over her body. It felt like a lovely whisper echoing down to the tops of her knees.

"You really do look nice in that dress," Brock said. "It brings out your eyes."

"Thank you," she said. "So does your tie."

He shot her a disbelieving glance. "Yeah, sure. My white shirt does amazing things for my eyes."

"Actually, it does," she said. "Because you're dark-complected. The white shirt provides a contrast against your complexion, and your blue tie emphasizes your blue eyes."

"So you say," he said with a shrug.

"One more thing that makes you hot," she said.

He did a double take. "Really?" he said.

"Yes, really," she responded. "With your tanned skin and dark hair, you're expecting brown eyes. Instead, yours are a shock. A compelling shock."

"Nice to know I have a genetic predisposition toward keeping you attracted," he said and extended his arm. "Ready to go?"

Just fifteen minutes later, Dirk pulled up in front of Carol's new condominium. A desk with security and a concierge stood just inside the beautiful building.

"By the price I paid, I knew Mummy wasn't slumming," Brock murmured as he showed his ID to security.

"Do you regret getting this place for her?" Elle asked,

knowing that she was a big part of the reason Brock had bought his mother the condo.

"Are you kidding? I would have paid twice as much to get her out of the house," he said as they stepped onto an elevator. "There's a reason I spent so many nights at the apartment. But you've made the house feel more like a home for me," he told Elle.

A warm feeling surged inside her. "I'm glad. I wanted to make you feel comfortable there."

The elevator dinged their arrival on Carol's floor. "Here we go," Brock said. He glanced at his watch. "Thirty minutes to go."

Less than a moment later, the door opened and a butler dressed in a tux greeted them. "Welcome to Mrs. Maddox's home. We're so glad for your presence. Please come in and enjoy the food, beverage and company."

From across the room, Brock's mother called out. "Brock, darling, bring your lovely wife here. I have some people I want her to meet."

"Warned you," Brock said under his breath as he slid his arm behind Elle's back.

"Hello, Mother," he said. "Your home is incredible," he said, looking around. "You never cease to amaze me with what you can do in such a short time."

Elle swallowed a chuckle, noticing his careful word choice. "I have to agree," she said. "It's amazing what you've accomplished."

Carol preened under the praise. "Thank you both. Of course, I've been working day and night to make this happen. I'd like you to meet my new neighbors, the Gladstones. Eve and Bill, this is my son Brock and my new daughter-in-law, Elle. Elle is going to give me a grandchild soon," she said in a stage whisper. "I'm so excited, I can't find the words."

Brock squeezed Elle's shoulders. "We're very excited, too, Mr. and Mrs. Gladstone. It's nice to meet you. I'm glad to know my mother has some wonderful neighbors."

"Nice to meet you," Elle said, extending her hand, a bit off-balance from Carol's announcement of her pregnancy.

"Our pleasure," Eve said. "And when is the little one due? Next year?"

Elle opened her mouth to reply, but Brock moved forward. "Again, nice to meet you." He nodded to his mother. "I'm going to get Elle something to drink," he said and guided Elle away. "Ready to go now?" he asked.

"It wasn't that bad," she said. "I just didn't expect her to mention the pregnancy."

"That's part of her charm. The unexpected," he said, lifting a glass of red wine from a server's tray. "Could you bring some sparkling water for my wife?" he asked the man.

The server nodded. "Just a moment," he said and swiveled to go to another room.

Brock glanced around. "Some of this stuff looks familiar."

"It should," Elle said. "She took some of it with her."

"But she sent me an astronomical bill for decorating," he said.

Elle shrugged. "Sorry. Not my area. I'm accustomed to shopping at outlets."

"And I'll take you away from all that," Brock said, his expression softening.

"I hope not," she said. "There's nothing wrong with taking a pause before you spend a lot of money."

He tilted his head to one side. "How refreshing," he said.

The waiter returned with a glass of fizzy water. "Here you go, miss."

"Thank you," Elle said to the man. "She hired excellent staff," she murmured after he left.

"As if my mother would have done anything else," Brock said with dark humor.

"Brock, it's been so long," a feminine voice said from behind them.

Elle glanced at Brock's face as she turned and saw his expression twist in pain just before it shuttered and went blank. "Claire," he said in the most neutral voice Elle had ever heard him use. "What a surprise."

Elle looked at the tall, beautiful blonde with a perfect shape and felt a sinking sensation in her stomach. "Claire?" she echoed, searching her memory for the name and unfortunately coming upon it.

Claire was Brock's ex-fiancée.

Ten

The ravishing specimen of beauty flicked her gaze over Brock. "You're looking good," Claire purred. "I've missed you."

Elle bristled at the woman's obvious seductive tone.

"I didn't know you and my mother were still in touch," Brock said.

"She insisted I come tonight. She told me you would be here."

Brock cleared his throat. "Claire, this is my wife, Elle."

Claire blinked and parted her lips as if in surprise. "I thought I'd heard a rumor, but I wasn't sure," she said in a sad voice, then turned to Elle. "Congratulations, Elle. You got a wonderful man."

"I know," Elle said, forcing herself to extend her hand. "Thank you. Lovely to meet you."

"She's so sweet," Claire said to Brock. "I never would have expected you to choose someone so—" She broke off and shrugged her bare, glimmering shoulders. "It's coming back to me now. Are the two of you expecting?"

Silence stretched between them, against the background noise of social conversation and tinkling glasses.

"Yes," Brock said. "Elle and I are very much looking forward to our first child."

Claire stared into Brock's eyes and her gaze seemed to say, *I could have been the mother of your child instead of her.* Claire nodded. "Congratulations. How exciting," she said. "I see an old friend. Please excuse me."

"Of course," Brock said and took a long swallow of wine. "I'm ready to go."

"Me, too," Elle said, every bit of social courteousness sucked out of her.

Brock's mother stepped in front of them just as they approached the door. "Leaving so soon? You just arrived," she said with a practiced pout.

"Perhaps if you hadn't invited my ex-fiancée and also neglected to tell her that I'm married, we might have stayed five minutes longer," Brock said, clenching his jaw in obvious anger.

Elle's stomach began to churn. She didn't know what upset her more—Brock's fury, his mother's manipulation or the memory of Brock's stunning ex-fiancée.

Carol's eyes rounded in mock innocence. "But I

thought you two would enjoy seeing each other. Time to let bygones be bygones now that you're married," she said, shooting a glance at Elle before she looked at Brock again. "Unless it stirred up old feelings—"

Elle swallowed a gasp.

"Not from me," Brock said. "The only thing you're stirring up is trouble. You invited Claire to intimidate Elle."

Carol shook her head. "Oh, now, really. How could Claire intimidate Elle?"

"Exactly," Brock said. "Elle is my wife and the mother of my child. Claire is history. You might want to remember that. Good night," he said, and ushered Elle through the door.

Fifteen minutes later, Elle and Brock walked inside the house. The housekeeper greeted them. "May I get something for you?"

"No, thank you," Brock said.

"I'm fine," Elle said.

"Are you sure you wouldn't like some sparkling water?" Anna asked with a gentle smile.

"No, thank you," Elle said, feeling as if she'd lost every bit of her sparkle. "I'll just get a bottle upstairs. You're kind to ask, though. Thank you."

She and Brock climbed the stairs and Elle stared into the mirror as she removed her earrings and necklace. She felt like such a fool. She'd tried so hard to look pretty, but Brock's ex was at a totally different level. The woman was breathtaking.

"You okay?" Brock asked.

"She could be a model," Elle said.

"That doesn't mean she was right for me."

"But she was perfect, gorgeous. I bet she's intelligent. You wouldn't tolerate anything less. How could—"

"She was extremely demanding. I knew it wouldn't work," he said.

Her heart sank to her knees. Elle turned to him. "And I'm not demanding," she said. "I'm grateful. So maybe it will work."

"Elle, come on, this is exactly what my mother wanted you to worry about," Brock said, walking toward her.

She put her hands out in front of her. "No, no. I need a few moments. Hours, maybe." She shook her head and fought the pain that wrenched inside her. "I know you married me because I got pregnant. But are you really counting on me to be the grateful little wife who doesn't ask too much of you?"

"Of course not," he said. "You always challenged me. That was part of the reason I couldn't resist you. You affected me that way from the beginning. I broke all my rules for you, Elle. If I'd followed my own policies, I would have had you transferred. But being with you made me feel like...I'd found home." He shrugged. "You can believe me or not. It's your choice."

She stared into his face and saw the raw truth. He loved her, even if he couldn't say it yet. It shocked and comforted her at the same time. "I believe you," she whispered, and flew into his arms.

He held her tight. "Listen, the next two weeks will be a crunch. But after that, you and I will take a break and go away."

"The mountain cabin?" she asked.

"Anywhere you want," he said and pressed his mouth

against hers. He slid his hand to her belly. "I never had so much to live for before," he said. "How'd I manage this?"

"You got lucky," she said and smiled.

"Yeah, I did."

Brock breezed through his morning, accomplishing tasks far faster than usual. Lunchtime came and he called Elle. She was eating a sandwich with her mom and planned to visit her grandfather that afternoon.

The latter gave him a twinge, but he ignored it. "I'll see you tonight," he said.

"Don't work too hard," she said, and the smile in her voice flooded him with warmth.

He roared through the afternoon. The only thing that stopped him was the sight of Logan Emerson walking into his office with a solemn expression on his face. "There's been a leak."

"About what?" Brock demanded, frustration soaring through him. He'd already eliminated one threat. What else could be at work here?

"The Prentice account," Logan said. "Someone got your files and shared them with Golden Gate."

Brock frowned. "I still don't understand what information you're talking about."

"Did you take anything home?" Logan asked.

"A flash drive and one file, three weeks ago," Brock said.

Logan lifted one brow. "Enough to give Golden Gate an edge."

Brock pictured the flash drive and file sitting on his

desk at home, right after he and Elle had gotten married. His stomach fell to his feet.

Elle put the final stamp of approval on dinner, which consisted of Brock's favorite red wine, beef burgundy, potatoes, broccoli and bread. Even though one of the staff would gladly do it, she lit the candles on the table and arranged the roses herself. She had never felt more hopeful, more in love. Maybe, just maybe, it would all work out. Her heart skipping a beat, she took a deep breath and laughed at herself. *Calm down,* she told herself. This was just another night of married life. The best kind of married life, a little voice inside her said.

She heard the sound of footsteps and her heart raced again. Brock was home. She looked up, unable to keep from beaming at him. "Welcome home," she said.

His face was blank, but anger blazed in his eyes. His mouth was set with bitterness, his jaw clenched. "When did you tell your grandfather about the new plans for the Prentice account?" he asked.

Elle felt her blood drain to her feet. She shook her head. "What are you talking about?"

"Weeks ago, I brought home a file and a flash drive. I left it here for one day. One day," he repeated. "Convenient for you."

"I have no idea what you're talking about, Brock," she said.

"There's no need to lie. You've got me. You've got our marriage. It's not as if I can do anything about the fact that you stole information from me again. I just want to know when you did it. That's fair, isn't it?"

Elle felt nauseous. "I didn't tell anyone anything

after that day you came to my mother's house. I don't know what you're talking about. You wouldn't even discuss the new Prentice campaign with me. Don't you remember?"

"I remember," he said. "I also remember I made the huge mistake of leaving work at home. I'm sure that would have been too tempting for you to resist."

Elle shook her head. "You're wrong. I didn't even see that file or your flash drive. And if I had, I wouldn't have touched them. I couldn't stand any more deception. I wanted things to be clean and honest between you and me. You have to believe me. You have to."

"Why should I believe you now?" he asked. "You spent months deceiving me while you went to bed with me. I'm starting to wonder if the pregnancy wasn't some part of your plan. If you tied yourself to me with a child, I couldn't possibly prosecute you. Right?"

Elle lifted her hand to her throat, feeling it close, nearly depriving her of oxygen. She shook her head. "Brock, you can't possibly think that. Not about our baby. Not about me."

His gaze dipped to her still-small belly. "I know that when it came to a test of your loyalties, you chose your grandfather."

"No, I chose my mother," she cried. "What else could I do? Can you honestly tell me that if your father had been ill and you had been put in the same situation, that you wouldn't have done the same thing I did?"

"I would never have been in your situation because I would have made sure I was never at someone else's mercy like that," he said.

Elle gasped at his words. Somewhere beneath her

pain, anger roared to the surface. "Well, how nice for you that you've never been vulnerable. How nice that you were born to privilege, educated at only the best schools and eased into a high-profile job."

"I fought for that job," Brock said. "My father didn't give me any passes for my work at Maddox."

"Like I said, good for you," she said. "I'll tell you this much. If I had it to do all over again, I would make the same horrible choice because my mother's life depended on it. I'm sorry I hurt you because I did fall in love with you. Helplessly, hopelessly. Then the pregnancy took me by surprise."

He stared at her without an ounce of compassion. "It's convenient for you to bring up love at this point when you've never mentioned it before," he said. "I'm staying at the apartment tonight. Congratulations on fooling me twice, Elle. Sleep well. It must be nice to be able to lie and sleep as easily as you do." Then he turned and walked out.

The knot of emotion in her throat threatened to choke her. She wanted to call after him and defend herself, but her voice completely failed. How could he believe she had gone behind his back again?

Because she'd done it before, just as he'd said. For months.

So why should he believe her? What evidence had she given him to believe the contrary? The answer made her so nauseous she dashed to the bathroom and was sick to her stomach. Leaning against the sink, she rinsed her mouth and pressed a cool, wet cloth to her head.

She put herself in Brock's place. With their history, would she have believed him?

Even though she knew in her heart of hearts that she loved Brock and would never deceive him again, she could see why he wouldn't believe her. The reality made her eyes burn and her chest hurt as if someone had torn out her heart. A sob bubbled up from somewhere deep inside her and she began to cry huge, wrenching sobs. She cradled her arms around her chest to hold herself together, but she felt as if she were splitting apart.

Of all the things she'd had in her life, she'd lost the most important. The promise, the dream of something different for her and Brock and their baby.

Elle didn't eat one bite that night. She couldn't have forced it down her throat. She was in such terrible emotional pain and shock that she didn't know what to do. Should she leave? Should she stay?

She took a hot, calming shower, dressed in a soft nightshirt and crawled into bed in Brock's room. She could still smell just a trace of his scent when she closed her eyes. A tidal wave of memories swept over her and she couldn't stop herself from crying again. She'd thought there wasn't one more tear she could shed tonight, but she was wrong. Finally, she exhausted herself and fell asleep.

Awakening in the morning with swollen eyes, she immediately remembered everything that had happened the previous night and pulled the sheet over her head. Was there any way she could turn back time and fix everything?

Not unless she was a genie or a witch. Brock seemed bent on believing she was the latter. She pulled back the sheet and gazed out the windows. Another gray, foggy morning in San Francisco. Natives knew the truth about the bay's climate. Fog, fog and more fog. She slid out of the bed and peeked through the blinds at the gray day.

Her heart still hurt as if she'd had major surgery. Biting her lip, she knew she needed to figure out what to do. If Brock despised her as much as he seemed, then he would never trust her. What kind of marriage could they have? What kind of parents would they be together?

Elle refused to have the same kind of relationship with Brock that his parents had appeared to have. That couldn't be good for anyone. No matter what happened between her and Brock, at least the baby would have a father. That was more than she'd ever had.

Her mind was spinning and she couldn't stop it. Scenario after scenario flew through her mind. What would she do? How would she live? She didn't mind going back to work. In this situation, she would welcome it. But would Brock try to take the baby from her? She'd never, ever let that happen.

Her stomach growled despite the fact that she couldn't imagine eating. She needed to eat, she told herself, for the baby if nothing else. She took another shower in hopes of cleansing herself of the dirty feeling that covered her like a veil of pollution.

Possibilities, choices chugging through her mind, she went downstairs. The housekeeper greeted her with a concerned expression. "Is everything okay? Your meal was left untouched."

"Mr. Maddox had a crisis at work," Elle said and heaven knew it was the truth.

"Oh, what a shame," the housekeeper said, folding

her hands in front of her sympathetically. "Can I get you anything for breakfast?"

"Thank you," Elle said. "I'd like something bland. Toast and jelly."

"I'll bring a scrambled egg on the side and some oatmeal just in case. Perhaps a little fruit," the house-keeper continued. "And just a couple of slices of bacon. Protein for the little one."

Although her stomach seemed the size of a pea, Elle managed to down a few bites of egg, toast and even a strip of bacon. She swallowed several sips of icy fresh-squeezed orange juice and said a mental goodbye to the notion of having staff at her beck and call. That wasn't the worst of her losses, she knew.

She decided to explain her plans to the housekeeper later, after she had packed. Upstairs, on the bed she'd shared with Brock, she pulled out two suitcases and began to put clothes inside. She found a box for her favorite books and keepsakes she'd brought from her mother's.

She heard the doorbell ring but ignored it. Elle knew she couldn't stay under the circumstances. Brock would never trust her and she wouldn't subject him, her or her baby to the life of misery their enforced togetherness would create. She wouldn't be able to bear his bitterness and resentment and the effect of his hatred of her on their child. The thought of it wrenched at her again.

"Oh, hello," Brock's mother said from the doorway. "Anna said you were napping, but I heard sounds. I hope you don't mind that I came upstairs," Carol said. "I just wanted to thank you and Brock for attending my little open house the other night." Carol stopped, finally taking in the sight of Elle's suitcases and boxes. "Oh, my goodness, you're not packing, are you?"

Elle bit the inside of her lip. "Brock and I have realized we're not well suited, so I've decided it's best if I leave."

"Oh, dear," Carol said, her voice oozing sympathy. "I'm so very sorry." She walked into the room, dressed in her couture of the day. "But I totally understand. Not everyone is cut out to be the wife of a Maddox. I'm not sure I really was, either," Carol confessed in a soft voice. "If I'd known in the beginning what I learned just after a year, I'm not sure I would have—" She broke off and shrugged. "Well, you know what I'm saying. Can I help you pack?"

Elle blinked at the woman's offer. "Uh—"

"I'm sure it's difficult for you," Carol said, moving to Elle's side and picking up a book. "Is this yours?"

"Yes," Elle said, watching as she put the book in a box.

"I'm so sorry that things didn't work out with you and Brock, but again, I understand," Carol said. "Between the Prentice account and the threat from Golden Gate, Brock just can't see straight. It seems the Prentice account is a twenty-four-hour-a-day job. Maddox is always having to come up with a new campaign."

Elle's antennae went on alert. "New campaign for Prentice?" she asked, pasting a bland look on her face. "What was wrong with the old one?"

"With an account like Prentice, they're always demanding something new. Brock's most recent idea may cost some bucks, though," Carol said, picking up a stuffed monkey. "Is this yours?"

"From my mother," Elle said. "I've had him since I was a child."

"How sweet," Carol said and put the monkey in the box. "Is this everything?"

"Not quite," Elle said. "I'm curious. How did you hear about the new campaign for Prentice? I didn't know a thing about it."

For a microsecond Carol froze as if she knew she'd been caught. Then she shrugged. "I thought everyone knew."

"Of course everyone didn't know," Elle said, her anger growing. "Only someone who'd looked at Maddox's plans would know about the changes. Only someone who'd had a chance to look at papers and a flash drive left at home by the Maddox CEO."

Carol gasped. "Whatever are you saying?"

"Hello, Mother," Brock said from the doorway, shocking Elle with his entrance. She gaped at him, wondering what had made him return home so early. He shot a glance at her full of forgiveness and repentance that made her heart turn over.

"Why, hello, Brock," Carol said with forced happiness. "What a surprise."

"You were the one," he said, walking toward his mother.

Carol gave a one-shoulder shrug and steadied herself on an end table. The woman suddenly appeared frail to Elle. "What are you talking about?"

"You looked at my file. You made a copy of my flash drive," he said.

Carol shrugged again, but this time she backed away. "What's that? What file?"

"The file for the Prentice account. You sent it to Golden Gate," he said. "You wanted me to believe Elle sent it, but all along, it was you."

"It could have been her. She lied to you before you married her. She could have brought down Maddox Communications," Carol said, her eyes glinting with fear and fury.

"Why did you do this?" he demanded. "It would only hurt you in the end."

"I knew you would find a way to top Golden Gate Promotions, but your marriage was ruining my future. Look at what it's already done to me. I've moved into a small condo! And I know the terms of your father's will. My income has been cut as a result of your bastard child."

Elle stared at the woman in shock. How could one person hold so much vindictiveness and evil? She almost couldn't comprehend it.

Brock's eyes blazed with fury, but his voice was deadly calm. "I'm done with you. I never want to see you again. You won't get one more penny from me. I'm sorry you've turned into such a bitter woman, but I won't have you contaminating my marriage. Now, get out."

Carol narrowed her eyes at him in impotent rage, then stomped from the room. Her heavy footsteps echoed down the stairs and the sound of a door slamming vibrated throughout the house.

Brock took a deep breath and looked at Elle. "I was wrong."

Elle nearly laughed. "You think so?"

He walked toward her. "I am so very, very sorry. I

should have believed you and from now on, I will," he promised.

Elle tore her gaze from his to glance at her luggage, trying to hang on to her plan to move away from him and make a new life for her baby and herself. "We have so much baggage," she whispered. "How can you ever trust me?"

"I already do," he said. "I trusted you when I shouldn't have. When I was told by a professional that you were deceiving me."

"What do you mean?"

"I forced the P.I. to give me evidence that you were selling secrets to Golden Gate. Not until he provided me with ironclad proof did I believe it."

Elle felt her eyes burn with tears. "I hate it that I lied to you. I hate myself for it."

"You need to forgive yourself," Brock said. "I forgive you."

Elle looked up, searching his gaze. "How can you?"

"Because I know you were doing the best you could. I know you were tortured about it," he said.

"I was," she agreed. "When I met you, I fell so hard for you. In my grandfather's plan, everything was supposed to remain business, but you blew me away. You were everything I'd wished for in a man, but had never found."

"And you were everything I wanted in a woman, but felt I'd never find. When I made love to you, I felt like I was coming home," Brock said, pulling her into his arms. "I never knew what love was before I met you."

Elle's heart stopped in her chest. "Love?"

He nodded. "Love. I was willing to risk it all for you. Even Maddox Communications. Logan tried to talk me into prosecuting, but I refused. It wasn't just about the baby. It was about the connection you and I shared. I knew I'd never find that again. When you told me that you'd agreed to spy for your grandfather so that your mother would get her treatments, I could only hope you felt that strongly about me."

"I do," Elle said. "I would do anything for you, Brock. I love you. More than anything. I want to build a life together."

"Then stay," he said, pressing his mouth against hers. "Stay forever."

Epilogue

The jazz band played in the background of the Maddox Communications party. They were celebrating the merger of Maddox and Golden Gate Promotions with Brock as the CEO. Elle slid a hand behind her grandfather's back and gave him a hug. He felt so frail to her. "Are you okay?" she asked.

Her grandfather smiled. "It was meant to be. Your husband is the future of both Maddox Communications and Golden Gate Promotions. My sons didn't have the drive, but Brock, he does."

Elle glanced at Brock across the room as he chatted with his brother and felt a rush of love. Their relationship had grown by leaps and bounds during the last few weeks.

"I should sit down," her grandfather said.

"Of course," she said, feeling remiss. "Can I get you something else to drink?"

"This water is fine," he said and nodded as he sat. "Go see to your guests."

Elle dropped a kiss on his forehead. For all the pain and suffering Athos had caused, he had led her to Brock and she was thankful for that. She had walked just a few steps when she was stopped by Evan and Celia Reese.

"How is life with the CEO of the newly merged Maddox Communications and Golden Gate Promotions?" Evan asked. "Are you keeping him in line?"

"Ha," Elle said, but smiled because Brock had made a special point to spend more time with her lately. "You two look like you're doing great. I'm so happy you could come to the party."

"Wouldn't miss it," Celia said, pushing her red hair behind her ear as she gazed affectionately at her husband. "This is actually a stopover. We're going to the French Riviera. Evan is determined to give me a honeymoon I'll never forget."

"It's hard being married to an overachiever, isn't it?" Elle joked.

Celia laughed. "You bet. Good luck with the baby."

"Thanks," Elle said and moved toward Brock. She noticed he and his brother were looking intently at their cell phones.

"What are they doing?" Elle asked as Flynn's wife appeared at her side.

"It's the battle of the ultrasounds," Renee said. "We may know the sex of our baby, but yours is set to disco. I think it's a draw."

Elle laughed. "How are you feeling?" she asked.

"Excited," Renee said, stroking her full pregnancy bump. "The doctor says my due date will be here before I know it, but it feels like forever."

"Any names yet?" Elle asked.

"We're still playing with the first name, but I want Flynn for her middle name," Renee said.

"I love that," Elle said.

Renee nodded. "It's good, isn't it? What about you and Brock?"

"We find out the sex for sure at the end of this week. If it's a boy, we'll include Brock's father's name somehow," she said.

Renee tilted her head. "Your mother looks great."

Elle's heart squeezed tight as she looked at her mother standing several feet away, tapping her foot as she enjoyed the party and the music. "Thank you. She's come a long way."

"There are our brides," Flynn interjected, clinking his beer against Brock's beer bottle. "We did good, didn't we?"

Brock met Elle's gaze and she felt a melting sensation. "I couldn't agree more," he said. "I won the ultrasound contest."

"That's a lie," Flynn said. "I know the sex and my baby is going to beat you to the punch."

Before Brock could dispute his brother, Jason Reagert and his very pregnant wife, Lauren, approached them. "If we're going to talk about winning the time game, Lauren and I will beat both of you," Jason, newly promoted to vice president, said.

Lauren, in her ninth month of pregnancy, glowed

with love and happiness. "That's right," she said. "Our baby boy could make his appearance any minute."

"Stop making me nervous," Brock said. "Do we have a doctor in the crowd?"

"Trust me. I'm on the edge of my seat," Jason said. "I have a packed bag for her sitting in the car."

Gavin Spencer, the former ad executive for Maddox who had started his own business, stepped forward and extended his hand. "Congratulations," Gavin said. "I can only hope I'll give you some competition in the future."

Brock gave a loud chuckle. "You dog."

Bree smiled at her husband. "Don't underestimate Gavin," she said.

"Or you," Brock said. "Elle tells me you helped with redecorating the house. Thanks," he said.

"My pleasure," Bree said.

Brock took a deep breath and exhaled, squeezing Elle's shoulders. She could feel his excitement emanate from his body, and she knew that when all was said and done, he would come home to her, seeking her love and affection. The knowledge made her feel more complete than she'd ever dreamed.

"It's time for a toast," Brock said as someone dinged a spoon against a crystal champagne flute. It took several moments, but silence finally descended over the crowd. "This has been a long time coming," Brock said. "Golden Gate Promotions has been a jewel in the crown of San Francisco ad agencies, always raising the bar for their competitors. I'm pleased to announce the merger of Golden Gate Promotions and Maddox Communications. The combined force of the two companies will create an unbeatable alliance of power and talent. To Athos Koteas," Brock said, lifting his glass to the man seated on the other side of the room. "I will always honor your spirit of creativity. To my father, I will always honor the gift of Maddox Communications that he built from the ground up. To my wife, Elle," he said, taking her by surprise.

She blinked at him.

"Yes, you," he said. "You have given my life meaning beyond work. You have given me a home whenever I'm with you. I love you."

Elle's eyes filled with tears. "I love you, too," she whispered.

The room echoed with applause.

"Hear, hear," Asher Williams, CFO of Maddox Communications said. "Melody and I have some news, too," he said, pulling his lovely wife against him. "We're having twins."

The group crowed with approval and applauded again.

"Congratulations," Brock said, extending his hand. "You've been busy."

"No more than you," Ash said with a broad smile.

Walter Prentice, Maddox's star client, stepped forward and patted Brock on the back. "You're doing a good job. More than ever, I can tell we signed with the right firm."

"I'm glad you feel that way," Brock said. "We'll work to make sure you continue to feel that way. Mrs. Prentice," Brock said, nodding toward Walter's wife. "Thank you for coming tonight."

Angela looked strained and unhappy, which was

highly unusual for Walter's beloved wife. "Congratulations on your success," she said. "And on the baby. Never underestimate the importance of your wife and children."

Brock sensed a sadness beneath the surface, but he knew now wasn't the time to comment. Instead, he took her hand in his. "I won't," he said earnestly.

Brock felt his brother, Flynn, draw him aside. "Excuse me," he said to Angela.

"We have something else to toast," Flynn said, giving his brother a fresh beer.

"What?" Brock asked.

"Who isn't here tonight?" Flynn asked. "Who is missing?"

Brock glanced around the busy room and shrugged. "I don't know. Who?"

"Mother," Flynn said with a dry smile.

"Oh, my God, you're right," Brock said.

"Renee tells me she has found a man willing to keep her in the style to which she has become accustomed," Flynn said.

"How could we possibly get that lucky?" Brock asked.

"I don't know, but I refuse to question good fortune." He bumped his bottle against Brock's again. "Ding-dong, the witch—"

"Is gone," Brock said and slapped his brother on the back. "I never would have pictured this last year. Would you?"

Flynn shook his head. "Some things turn out better than you expect," he said.

Brock latched his gaze onto Elle as she walked

toward him. She was his home. He'd never known true love until her. Thank God he'd found her. "Better than I could have dreamed," Brock said and opened his arms to his wife.

"Are you having a good night?" she asked, smiling up at him.

"I'm having a good life," he said. "Because of you."

* * * * *

COMING NEXT MONTH

Available July 13, 2010

#2023 THE MILLIONAIRE MEETS HIS MATCH
Kate Carlisle
Man of the Month

#2024 CLAIMING HER BILLION-DOLLAR BIRTHRIGHT
Maureen Child
Dynasties: The Jarrods

#2025 IN TOO DEEP
"Husband Material"—Brenda Jackson
"The Sheikh's Bargained Bride"—Olivia Gates
A Summer for Scandal

#2026 VIRGIN PRINCESS, TYCOON'S TEMPTATION
Michelle Celmer
Royal Seductions

#2027 SEDUCTION ON THE CEO'S TERMS
Charlene Sands
Napa Valley Vows

#2028 THE SECRETARY'S BOSSMAN BARGAIN
Red Garnier

REQUEST YOUR FREE BOOKS!

2 FREE NOVELS
PLUS 2
FREE GIFTS!

Passionate, Powerful, Provocative!

YES! Please send me 2 FREE Silhouette Desire® novels and my 2 FREE gifts (gifts are worth about $10). After receiving them, if I don't wish to receive any more books, I can return the shipping statement marked "cancel." If I don't cancel, I will receive 6 brand-new novels every month and be billed just $4.05 per book in the U.S. or $4.74 per book in Canada. That's a saving of at least 15% off the cover price! It's quite a bargain! Shipping and handling is just 50¢ per book.* I understand that accepting the 2 free books and gifts places me under no obligation to buy anything. I can always return a shipment and cancel at any time. Even if I never buy another book, the two free books and gifts are mine to keep forever.

225/326 SDN E5QG

Name	(PLEASE PRINT)	
Address		Apt. #
City	State/Prov.	Zip/Postal Code

Signature (if under 18, a parent or guardian must sign)

Mail to the Silhouette Reader Service:

IN U.S.A.: P.O. Box 1867, Buffalo, NY 14240-1867
IN CANADA: P.O. Box 609, Fort Erie, Ontario L2A 5X3

Not valid for current subscribers to Silhouette Desire books.

Want to try two free books from another line?
Call 1-800-873-8635 or visit www.morefreebooks.com.

* Terms and prices subject to change without notice. Prices do not include applicable taxes. N.Y. residents add applicable sales tax. Canadian residents will be charged applicable provincial taxes and GST. Offer not valid in Quebec. This offer is limited to one order per household. All orders subject to approval. Credit or debit balances in a customer's account(s) may be offset by any other outstanding balance owed by or to the customer. Please allow 4 to 6 weeks for delivery. Offer available while quantities last.

Your Privacy: Silhouette Books is committed to protecting your privacy. Our Privacy Policy is available online at www.eHarlequin.com or upon request from the Reader Service. From time to time we make our lists of customers available to reputable third parties who have a product or service of interest to you. If you would prefer we not share your name and address, please check here. ☐

Help us get it right—We strive for accurate, respectful and relevant communications. To clarify or modify your communication preferences, visit us at www.ReaderService.com/consumerschoice.

SDES10R

HARLEQUIN®

A Romance

FOR EVERY MOOD™

Spotlight on

— Heart & Home —

Heartwarming romances
where love can happen
right when you least expect it.

See the next page to enjoy a sneak peek
from Silhouette Special Edition®,
a Heart and Home series.

Introducing McFARLANE'S PERFECT BRIDE
by USA TODAY *bestselling author Christine Rimmer,*
from Silhouette Special Edition®.

Entranced. Captivated. Enchanted.

Connor sat across the table from Tori Jones and couldn't help thinking that those words exactly described what effect the small-town schoolteacher had on him. He might as well stop trying to tell himself he wasn't interested. He was powerfully drawn to her.

Clearly, he should have dated more when he was younger.

There had been a couple of other women since Jennifer had walked out on him. But he had never been entranced. Or captivated. Or enchanted.

Until now.

He wanted her—*her,* Tori Jones, in particular. Not just someone suitably attractive and well-bred, as Jennifer had been. Not just someone sophisticated, sexually exciting and discreet, which pretty much described the two women he'd dated after his marriage crashed and burned.

It came to him that he...he *liked* this woman. And that was new to him. He liked her quick wit, her wisdom and her big heart. He liked the passion in her voice when she talked about things she believed in.

He liked *her.* And suddenly it mattered all out of proportion that she might like him, too.

Was he losing it? He couldn't help but wonder. Was he cracking under the strain—of the soured economy, the McFarlane House setbacks, his divorce, the scary changes in his son? Of the changes he'd decided he needed to make in his life and himself?

Strangely, right then, on his first date with Tori Jones, he didn't care if he just might be going over the edge. He was having a great time—having *fun*, of all things—and he didn't want it to end.

Is Connor finally able to admit his feelings to Tori,
and are they reciprocated?
Find out in M<small>C</small>FARLANE'S PERFECT BRIDE
by USA TODAY *bestselling author Christine Rimmer.*
Available July 2010,
only from Silhouette Special Edition®.

HARLEQUIN Presents®

Bestselling Harlequin Presents® *author*

Penny Jordan

brings you an exciting new trilogy...

Needed:
THE WORLD'S MOST
ELIGIBLE
BILLIONAIRES

Three penniless sisters:
how far will they go to save the ones they love?

Lizzie, Charley and Ruby refuse to drown in their debts.
And three of the richest, most ruthless men in the world
are about to enter their lives. Pure, proud but penniless,
how far will these sisters go to save the ones they love?

Look out for

Lizzie's story—**THE WEALTHY GREEK'S**
CONTRACT WIFE, July

Charley's story—**THE ITALIAN DUKE'S**
VIRGIN MISTRESS, August

Ruby's story—**MARRIAGE: TO CLAIM HIS TWINS,**
September

Silhouette Desire

USA TODAY bestselling author

MAUREEN CHILD

brings you the first
of a six-book miniseries—

Dynasties: The Jarrods

Book one:

CLAIMING HER BILLION-DOLLAR BIRTHRIGHT

Erica Prentice has set out to claim
her billion-dollar inheritance
and the man she loves.

*Available in July
wherever you buy books.*

Always Powerful, Passionate and Provocative.